Rising Star

Samantha Alexander lives in Lincolnshire with a variety of animals including her thoroughbred horse, Bunny, and a pet goose called Bertie. Her schedule is almost as busy and exciting as her plots – she writes a number of columns for newspapers and magazines, is a teenage agony aunt for BBC Radio Leeds and in her spare time she regularly competes in dressage and showjumping.

*Also by Samantha Alexander
and available from Macmillan*

RIDERS

HOLLYWELL STABLES

RIDERS

4

Rising Star

SAMANTHA ALEXANDER

MACMILLAN CHILDREN'S BOOKS

First published 1997 by
Macmillan Children's Books
a division of Macmillan Publishers Ltd
25 Eccleston Place, London SW1W 9NF
and Basingstoke

Associated companies throughout the world

ISBN 0 330 34536 2

1 3 5 7 9 8 6 4 2

A CIP catalogue record for this book is available from the British Library.

Phototypeset by Intype London Ltd
Printed by Mackays of Chatham plc, Chatham, Kent

For Tony.
For your friendship and support, and for
reminding me that life is, and should always be,
an adventure.

Samantha Alexander and Macmillan Children's Books would like to thank *Horse and Pony* magazine for helping us by running a competition to find our cover girl, Sally Johnson. Look out for more about the **Riders** and **Hollywell Stables** series in *Horse and Pony* magazine and find out more about Samantha by reading her agony column in every issue.

Macmillan Children's Books would also like to thank Chris White; and David Burrows and all at Sandridgebury Stables, especially Toby and his owner Sylvie.

And finally thanks to Angela Clarke from Ride-Away in Sutton-on-Forest, Yorkshire for providing the riding clothes, hats and boots featured on the covers.

CHARACTERS

Alexandra Johnson   Our heroine. 14 years old. Blonde, brown eyes. Ambitious, strong-willed and determined to become a top eventer. Owns Barney, a 14.2 hh dun with black points.

Ash Burgess   Our hero. 19 years old. Blond hair, blue eyes, flashy smile. Very promising young eventer. He runs the livery stables for his parents. His star horse is Donavon, a 16.2 hh chestnut.

Zoe Jackson   Alex's best friend. 14 years old. Sandy hair, freckles. Owns Lace, a 14.1 hh grey.

Camilla Davies   Typical Pony Club high-flyer. 15 years old. Owns The Hawk, a 14.2 hh bay.

Judy Richards   Ash's head groom and sometime girlfriend. 18 years old.

Eric Burgess   Ash's uncle. Around 50 years old. His legs were paralysed in a riding accident. He has a basset hound called Daisy.

Look out for the definition-packed glossary of horsey terms at the back of the book.

CHAPTER ONE

I spotted the advert immediately:

> FOR SALE: 16.2, *advanced event horse*
> *"Donavon". £12,000 ono.*

It couldn't be. It couldn't possibly . . .

I slammed the magazine down in a state of shock. Then I picked it up again all fingers and thumbs.

> *Due to unforeseen circumstances. For further*
> *details please telephone . . .*

Oh my God. It was. I was stunned. I couldn't believe it. Not Donavon, oh not sweet lovely Donavon.

"Alex, what is it? What on earth's the matter?" Judy, the head groom, waltzed into the tack room scraping back her peroxide blonde hair and examining her peeling suntan in the mirror. "Alex? Alex, say something – you've gone as white as a sheet!"

Zoe, my best friend, came in and I passed her the magazine.

"Never!" She stared down at the advertisement in horror. "Ash would never sell Donavon – he adores him. It's got to be a mistake."

I plonked myself down in a chair and dug my fingers into my mass of blonde hair. "But it's there in black and white. I just don't understand."

Zoe leaned back, rubbing her freckled snubby nose and snorting with hay fever. "What happened to the Olympic dream? Come to that matter, what happened to good plain honesty?"

Ash, nicknamed Flash Burgess, was nineteen and one of the most talented event riders in the country. He was also my boyfriend. We told each other everything. He wouldn't keep something like this from me. He couldn't.

"Well, here's your chance to find out." Zoe stood up, stretching her back, watching the huge cream Lambourn horsebox edge its way into the yard, past the muck heap and the feed room towards the main stable block. Judy was there like a shot.

Ash leapt out of the driver's seat, his gold, sun-bleached hair flopping forward as he strode purposefully towards the ramp. He was wearing the "I'm so sexy" T-shirt I'd bought for his birthday and a pair of tight black jods which made him look leaner than ever.

George, a huge bay, thundered down the ramp with his feet the size of soup plates, rolling his eyes which always meant he was starving. George had been bought as a scraggy four-year-old from a dealer in Ireland. He had two hay nets a night and special body-building supplements. He could clear a triple bar two strides out. Donavon followed, a 16.2 chestnut with a white stripe. He looked every inch a superstar in a smart navy rug as he strode towards the stable. How could Ash possibly sell him? He'd owned him since Donavon was eight months old.

"Be careful." Zoe caught my arm as I reached for the door handle. "You don't know the full facts. You don't know what's going on."

I burst through the office door like a tornado and threw the magazine down on the table half scrunched up at the relevant page.

"I thought we were supposed to be close," I lashed out. "I thought we told each other everything."

"Oh. I see."

"You – you mean it's true?" I stood back incredulous, wanting him to deny it, wanting him to say it was all some kind of crazy joke.

"I knew you'd find out sooner or later."

My jaw dropped. All I could do was stare into his languid blue eyes and wonder what on

3

earth he'd turned into. This wasn't the person I'd fallen in love with. That person didn't buckle at the knees at the slightest obstacle and decide to sell off his best horse.

"I've had enough, Alex. It's as simple as that. I can't carry on."

"Poppycock. There's no such word as 'can't'. You're being a wimp."

A few weeks ago Ash's sponsor had run into cash-flow problems and pulled out, leaving him high and dry. I knew there'd have to be cut-backs but I'd never imagined this. Judy had volunteered to take a wage cut even though she was on a pittance as it was. I'd been trying to drum up business by attempting to poach livery owners from the neighbouring riding school.

"You can't sell Donavon. You can't."

Ash leapt up and rattled open a filing cabinet, his hands trembling with fury. He pulled out a file and let a mountain of paperwork waft down onto the desk like confetti.

"Here, look at this: farrier's bill, two hundred and thirty pounds." He snatched at a yellow slip. "Vet's fees, one hundred and sixty, two months overdue. Woodshavings seventy-five pounds, entry fees ninety-five pounds. Do you want me to go on? Because believe me I could carry on all afternoon."

"There's no need to shout," I yelled back, trying to disguise the searing shock at the pile of

4

debt. "You've made your point. Can't you contact your parents?"

"No. It's a relief that they're in Australia. I don't want them to know that I've failed. They trusted me to run the business and I've let them down."

He flopped down in the chair again, his shoulders dropping, his eyes suddenly dulled with reality.

"Life isn't a bed of roses, Alex. It's tough and then it gets tougher. The last thing I need is a hard time from you."

I was swayed by his distress but then I thought of Donavon, standing in his stable, ready to try his heart out for Ash at the drop of a hat.

"I'd never sell Barney," I said. "Not if I had to starve. There are certain things you just never do."

Barney was my 14.2 hands dun, who made up for what he lacked in looks in guts and personality. I'd bought him for a song and he was blasting his way to the top.

"You can't take emotion to the bank." Ash was almost white from the strain. The weight had been dropping off him lately so his cheekbones stood out and his eye sockets were almost hollowed. "And while we're at it, there's a couple of other things you might as well know."

I pulled out the chair and sat down facing him knowing instinctively it wasn't good.

"I'm seriously thinking of pulling out of eventing altogether. I've been making inquiries about computer studies. There's a course starting in the next three weeks . . ."

"But Ash, you – you can't!"

"And I've just had a phone call. There's a girl on her way to see Donavon right now. I said she could try him on the manege."

I felt unbelievably sad.

"Judy's gone to pick up some saddle repairs. I . . . I . . ." His voice faltered, the stony facade starting to slip, revealing the real Ash. "I wondered if you could tack him up. I'm going for a walk."

He lunged for the door, a stifled sob catching in his throat. "Her name's Sasha. And make sure you tell her he loves flapjack."

I cast my eyes down on the desk where a message had been roughly scrawled on the back of an envelope. "Bank Manager. John Evans. Take in accounts. Badly overdrawn." There was a picture of a hangman's noose and the word "Help" written in a tilted bubble. Had things really got that bad?

CHAPTER TWO

"He's for sale?" Judy was shuddering from the shock of it. "Is Ash out of his mind?"

Zoe found some Lucozade in the fridge and poured out a glass.

"Here, this should help." She passed it to Judy who was grey with grief. Neat brandy would have been more appropriate.

"But he's my little baby – it will kill him to move from here. Ash knows how sensitive he is. How could he do this?"

She gripped my arm in desperation and then broke down in huge racking sobs. "I'll kill him." She looked up. "The traitor, the hard-hearted pig. How could he . . ."

"Judy, you don't know the full story. Ash is on the verge of going bust. The stables might go under."

She wiped her cheek and gaped at me in disbelief. "You mean I've been prancing round Minorca buying Kiss-me-quick hats and he's been facing the bailiff? Why didn't you tell me?"

"I didn't know. Nobody knew. It's a shock to all of us. I think he thought he could sort it out."

"I can't believe it. Wait till I get my hands on him."

Panic ripped through me with such force that I gripped her shoulders and wanted to shake her. "If you tell him," I almost screeched, "he'll finish with me. He might even ask me to move Barney. Judy, you've got to keep quiet. You've got to."

Her pale dove-grey eyes slowly melted as the anger slipped away. Judy was rash, passionate and dedicated to her horses but she wasn't stupid. Whatever we did to help would have to be behind Ash's back. Incognito.

"Well, he wants about twelve thousand for him."

"Great." Zoe chucked a chocolate wrapper at the waste-paper bin and missed. "I propose we start planning to rob a bank and change our names to Bonnie and Clyde."

"He's the most beautiful horse I've ever seen." Sasha Fennington gazed at Donavon with eyes practically on stalks.

She'd arrived on a bicycle with dodgy brakes carrying a riding hat and wearing jean jods and jodhpur boots.

Relief trickled through me like a hot drink on a cold day. There was no way Sasha had twelve thousand pounds to invest in a horse. She was obviously a professional sightseer; quite a few people made it their hobby to try out horses for sale with no intention of buying them. It gave them free rides and sometimes they struck lucky and managed to keep a horse on trial.

Sasha was obviously one of these types. She stared around the yard as if she'd never seen decent stables before. She was very thin, flat chested with a pretty face and huge green eyes.

"Is he always this good?"

Donavon stood like a police horse, his gleaming chestnut coat rippling in the sunlight, his beautifully sculptured head bent at the perfect angle.

"He's not a novice ride," I butted in, genuinely concerned that Sasha might not be able to ride him. "He's very highly trained, not your usual riding school horse."

"Oh, I can see that." Sasha moved forward running a hand down Donavon's forearm and along his near tendon. "You'd have to be a geek not to recognize quality like this." She lifted up the saddle flap and tightened the girth which I'd deliberately left loose. "So is it OK if I hop on?"

She was in the saddle before I'd even answered. Zoe altered the stirrups and I opened the gate to the manege. Reggie and Nigel, the two stable ducks and supposed lucky mascots, waddled out, fluttering their feathers at Donavon and making enough noise to wake the dead.

"You're so lucky to live in a place like this."

9

Sasha gathered up the reins, her eyes suddenly swimming with tears.

Zoe looked at me and I looked away, not knowing how to handle the situation.

"She's weird," Zoe hissed, as Donavon walked off round the edge of the ring.

"She can ride." I grabbed Zoe's arm in sudden panic.

Within minutes Donavon was purring round at trot, on a beautiful balanced stride, lengthening and shortening and turning up the middle in a dead straight line.

"Jesus," Zoe muttered. "She's brilliant!"

After about ten minutes she walked back to us on a loose rein and suggested some jumping. "I presume he's got no vices?"

"Oh yes." Zoe flung me a panicked look. "He crib-bites, he shies in traffic and he's a really bad doer."

"Well, it doesn't seem to affect his condition." Sasha leaned back and pressed her fingers on Donavon's rump. Donavon's back-end had a distinctive bump before it tapered off to his tail. This was always known as a "jumper's bump" and was a good sign of a horse's ability.

"I presume the price will take his crib-biting into consideration."

I glared at Zoe and dug her painfully in the

ribs as Sasha moved off towards the jumps.

"Nice one, brains. What are you going to suggest next, that he's not really Donavon at all?"

We were just debating as to who was going to put up the jumps when a metallic green Land Rover Discovery roared into the yard with Jasper Carrington behind the wheel waving and tooting wildly on the horn.

Toukie, his long-suffering girlfriend, fell out of the back seat along with Camilla. Both were wearing bikini tops and shorts together with knee pads, arm pads and carrying polo hats.

Jasper sprung out, waving a clutch of polo mallets.

"The kindergarten's about two miles up the road," I leered at Jasper in a voice dripping with acid.

"My dear, sexy, gorgeous Alex, when are you going to lighten up and become one of the gang?"

Camilla staggered forward. "We've h-had the most incredible time," she said. "You ought to have seen the guys."

Toukie proceeded to tell us how after the polo they'd been chucked out of the cinema for wolf-whistling every time Hugh Grant was on screen.

"You know, Alex, you look as poker-faced as Emma Thompson and you're only half her age. I'd be careful if I was you."

"Oh belt up," I yelled, furious that once again

11

they'd made a bad impression. The Sutton Vale Pony Club had had a two-day Polo training course at Sir Charles' establishment down the road. Six names had been drawn out of a hat and typically the three scrooges had come up trumps. Zoe and myself had missed out big time.

"I take it from your tone then that you're not yet willing to marry me?"

Jasper was a rich, spoilt hell-raiser and one of the biggest flirts in the county. Toukie only put up with him because every summer he took her on an expensive holiday. He was blond, too handsome for his own good and totally lacking in motivation.

"Don't tell me you're still love-sick for dear old Ash?"

"Can't you see we're busy?" I thundered, just wanting them to buzz off.

"I think not." Camilla took a swipe at Jasper's bottom with the largest mallet and burst into a fit of giggles. "Your little pupil's scarpered."

I spun round to see Donavon tied up to a fence post as good as gold, idly kicking up at the flies on his belly and swishing his tail.

"She's gone!" Zoe squeaked in disbelief.

Sasha Fennington had disappeared.

"Oh, I recognized her." Toukie lunged forward. "Didn't you know?" She suddenly became serious, "She's one of Sir Charles' grooms."

*

12

"It's bizarre." Zoe untacked Donavon, sliding off the saddle and numnah and putting on his summer sheet.

"She was just stirring." I strung up a full hay net and got seeds all down my shirt front. "Anyway, can anyone take notice of Toukie? She can't tell her left foot from her right!"

A stab of jealousy rent through me once again. What I wouldn't give to see Brooklands Training Centre. It was supposed to have an equine swimming pool, air-conditioned stables and at least ninety Polo ponies mainly shipped over from Argentina. Sir Charles was captain of the England Polo team and many people said he was so good with horses he could practically get them to talk. I didn't mind admitting it, I was green with envy. "I don't understand, though. Why would Sir Charles be interested in Donavon? Everybody knows Polo ponies are only 15.2. He's far too big."

"Yeah, but let's face it, old Charlie boy is one person who doesn't need to do the National Lottery. He could afford to have Donavon just for hacking."

"That's it!" I dropped the sweat scraper onto the concrete floor in unconcealed excitement. "Don't you see – the answer's staring us in the face."

Zoe looked vacant. "Alex, you're not making any sense."

"Oh yes I am." I grabbed at the stable door in a frenzy. "Well come on, you're the whiz kid at English. We need to write a begging letter."

The common room was a converted stable with a fridge, table, chairs, pool table and dart board. When we walked in, Camilla was sprawled at the table with three open bags of different flavoured crisps and a pen and paper. She was writing out twenty reasons why horse riding was cool which she was going to pin up on the school noticeboard.

I grabbed the pen and started pacing up and down for inspiration.

"Alex!"

"Believe me, Cam, this is a matter of life and death."

"What is?" Ash suddenly appeared in the doorway, glowering like a bull, towering above everyone. "Alex, a word please, outside – now."

He marched over to the hay barn picking up loose bits of baling string and cursing everyone within earshot.

"When I tell you something in private," he practically barked, "I expect it to stay that way, not to be spread all over the stables like the proverbial muck spreader."

"I haven't said a word." I desperately tried to look innocent. "I would never discuss your private business. Ever." I crossed my fingers behind my back and prayed I wouldn't be struck down by lightning.

"Oh no?" He raised his eyebrows in a perfect peak and shot me a quelling glance. "So, why is Judy in the bottom paddock crying her eyes out saying she'll stick by me no matter what? Does everybody know I've singlehandedly messed up my life? Or are you going to show some discretion? Let me guess, who's next on the list, the milkman, the blacksmith?"

"There's no need to be so nasty." I backed away, suddenly feeling as deflated as a pierced balloon. Red hot tears sprung from nowhere, spilling down my cheeks.

Ash looked about to explode. "Uuh, you've been caught out so now you're going for the Oscar. Terrific. Well done, Alex." His eyes narrowed into slits with rage.

"Oh, shut up," I bawled, my hands clenching into tight fists. "You always have to be so sarcastic." I twisted round, desperately making for the door, blinded by tears and streaked mascara. "I hate you."

Suddenly his hand clamped down on my elbow and he spun me round, hauling me into his arms. "Oh, Alex, I'm so sorry, I'm taking it out on you. Forgive me." He buried his head in my neck and wrapped his arms so tight round my waist I felt as if every breath of life was being pushed out.

"I feel such a failure, I just can't cope. If I lost you as well as Donavon . . ." He kissed my hair, my eyelids, my cheeks, and finally my mouth. I was just melting like butter on toast savouring the moment and wriggling even deeper into his arms.

"It's going to be OK," I croaked, trying to be strong. "It's always darkest before dawn – there's bound to be a solution." I wrapped my fingers into his thick gold hair and stood on tiptoe to kiss him. "We'll find an answer, we will, I promise you. But you've got to talk about it. You can't keep everything bottled up." I breathed in the musky scent of his aftershave mingled with horse and let his strength recharge me.

"I've just been speaking to the bank manager," he said. "Donavon's entered for Burnley – he's insisting I take him. Don't you see, Alex, it'll be our last competition together."

I grasped hold of his hands, hardly able to bear the pain in his eyes. He looked ravaged and desperate and defeated.

"Well then, there's only one thing you can do." I put his left hand against my cheek and tried to summon up every ounce of courage. I looked him straight in the eye and put on my most commanding voice. "You've got to win Burnley!"

CHAPTER THREE

"Get that yeller hoss out of my field before I shoot it." Mr Dawes, the local farmer, thrashed a walking stick crazily in the air, his fat red moon of a face looking about to explode. Barney charged past at a fast canter just far enough away to avoid injury, but close enough to send Mr Dawes into a rage. A field of ripening corn lay flattened and ruined.

I put my fingers in my mouth and whistled and within seconds Barney came storming up, a black muddy patch over one eye and a handful of corn dangling from his black mane and tail. His characteristic custard-yellow coat was speckled with dust and he reminded me of a chastised Labrador who'd gone off chasing rabbits.

"That hoss'll be the death of me." Mr Dawes waved his stick so that Barney flattened back his ears and gave him a glare that would have curdled milk. "Look at 'im, if I didn't know better I'd swear he were human."

Ever since a pretty Welsh Mountain mare had been turned out for the summer Barney kept jumping out of his field and going walkabout. He'd twice been caught at the local Half Moon pub supping Guinness from a builder's bucket and once nearly gave the cleaning lady at the church a heart attack when she spotted him lying flat out among the gravestones sunbathing. I slipped on his bridle and vaulted easily on to his bare back.

"I'll be getting in touch with your parents and if I see his ugly yeller face again I'll give 'em the address of the local glue factory."

"Whatever you think." I swallowed hard and resisted the temptation to be downright rude. I was sure that keeping an eye out for Barney's escape acts was giving Mr Dawes a new lease of life. Zoe said he'd even bought a pair of binoculars. "You may find this hard to believe, Mr Dawes, but one day in the not too distant future Barney is going to be famous."

"She's done what?"

Zoe turned off Radio One and repeated what she'd just told me very slowly.

I was standing in the stable yard, hosing Barney down. He was curling up his top lip and looking at me with disgust. There were soap suds everywhere.

"As far as I know," Zoe carried on, "she's in bed guzzling vitamin C and the doctor's ordered her to have a week off work."

Barney, who hated having the attention taken

18

off him for a second, plonked his hoof on the hosepipe and effectively cut off the water supply.

"They thought it might have been food poisoning but it looks like a virus. So much for ten days in Minorca."

Poor Judy. Apparently she'd been rushed off in Ash's jeep as grey as dishwater and clutching Donavon's feed bucket as a sick bag.

"Ash says to tell you he's pulling out of Burnley because he can't go without a groom, and that you're to respect his decision." Zoe wrinkled her nose as if she didn't know how I'd react. "The electricity man's been round and threatened to cut off the supply to the stables and what are we doing about this letter to Sir Charles? Alex?"

Despite the heat of the day I suddenly felt cold and flaky all over. I only knew one way in life and that was to lead from the front, to blast through obstacles and keep on going, no matter what. To achieve, to dream, to strike out for the top.

Zoe gently touched my arm, her voice filled with uncertainty. "Not everybody has your strength, you know, Alex. You can't judge other people by your own standards. You've got to let them find their own way."

I didn't answer. Very methodically, very mechanically, I put down the hosepipe and carefully unrolled my clinging wet sleeves. Then I tied

19

Barney's lead rope into a makeshift rein and for the second time that day vaulted nimbly onto his broad soapy back.

Zoe quailed visibly. "Alex, where on earth are you going now?" She blinked up at me, turning off the cold water tap.

I squeezed my heels into Barney's sides and swung him round towards the drive. "Something I should have done in the first place," I called back. "There's only one person in the whole world who can sort out this mess and that's Eric."

"I can't do anything." Eric Burgess turned his wheelchair away from the window, his face clamped with a stubborn determination.

The sunlight glinted through the window forming a shaft of light hovering with dust particles and focusing on a beautiful foxhunting oil painting above the fireplace.

"But you've got to help." I was undaunted. "You've got to – you love Donavon as much as anyone." I paced back and forth, momentarily thrown that he was being so blasé. He didn't even look surprised.

Eric Burgess was my trainer, my mentor, my best friend. He was also Ash's uncle. He was the only person who'd recognized that Barney had talent. Just a few months ago he'd set me a date exactly one year ahead when Barney would be at the National Championships. Since then he'd already won two one-day events and been labelled a bright hope for the future. Eric had turned Barney from an out-of-control maniac into a thinking, jumping machine and myself into a half-decent rider.

"He's going to pieces," I pleaded. "Having Donavon up for sale is ripping him apart."

I sank into an armchair feeling utterly drained and defeated. Eric had bred Donavon. He was the last colt from his favourite mare before she died. He'd watched every stage of his career from being backed to winning his first competition. I couldn't comprehend how he could stand by and let the worst happen.

"I can't help because Ash doesn't want my help. Because Ash has got to want to succeed for himself. It's got to come from him. So, there you have it." Eric turned and stared out of the window as if dismissing the whole matter.

"But he does want to succeed," I protested. "He doesn't want to sit in some crummy college. I know him. He's a rider – it's in his blood. It's in here." I thumped my chest, searching for the right words. "The least you could do is talk to him."

Aching minutes of complete silence edged by. Eric's dog, Daisy, wandered in from the kitchen, sucking her long basset hound ears and seeming quite oblivious to the tension.

21

A long time ago Eric and Ash had been sworn enemies. They hadn't spoken or seen each other for three years. Eric blamed Ash for his riding accident which had left him paralysed from the waist down. Ash was supposed to have been acting as groom at a major event but had failed to check the girth and over-surcingle which had snapped at a fence called Lover's Leap. Eric's back had been broken and the horse had to be put down due to a broken leg. It was horrific. Even more so because Ash had been drunk and accused Eric of putting him under too much pressure. It was all a terrible mess. Eric had never since advised Ash on his riding or his horses and Ash had never asked him.

"You know what I think." I stood up, lashing out verbally as a final resort. "I think you're both as stubborn as each other."

Eric finally looked away from the window, a deep gnawing sadness edged around his mouth. "Oh Alex, look at you, you're so young, so ideal-istic. When are you going to learn that you can't bulldoze people into doing what you want? They have to make their own decisions. Ash is nineteen. He's a young man in charge of his own life."

"And he's not going to wreck it, not if I can help it."

I marched across to the door feeling my neck flush and my determination scatter like confetti.

"If you really care about Ash," Eric suddenly

22

showed a real concern, "stand by him. He doesn't know it yet, but things are going to get worse. Much worse."

And then I realized that Eric Burgess knew far more than he was letting on.

Evening stables was chaotic. Without Judy the whole system of feeding and watering was turned upside down and by five o'clock half the horses still hadn't been fed. George, whose stomach came before anything else, had chewed up my favourite sweatshirt. Reggie and Nigel had waddled into the feed room and knocked over all of the soaked sugar beet; and Camilla had complained bitterly when we'd asked her to sort out her own horse and had demanded a ten per cent refund on her monthly payment. I gulped down a mug of cold tea pulling on a pair of mucker boots at the same time. Ash was in the barn getting bales of hay down.

I had a proposition and I had to make him listen. Just the thought of it made me tingle all over with excitement. Ash was right at the top of the stack, chucking bales around as if he was training for the Gladiators. The sweet delicious smell of meadow hay was almost overpowering as I finished my suggestion.

"So what do you think?"

Ash stared down at me, gently shaking his

head in disbelief. "I think it's time you took no for an answer."

I deliberately put on my best pouting look and didn't say anything, which always drove Ash mad. He said that at least while I was talking he knew where he was.

"Have you any idea what would be involved?"

I leapt in for the attack. "Sixteen miles of roads and tracks, two miles of steeplechase, a four mile cross-country, dressage and showjumping, three days of hardly any sleep. Endless worry. Putting up with your temper tantrums. I know I can do it."

"You're a masochist."

"A realist. If you get noticed you might not have to sell Donavon."

"We're not going to Burnley."

"You're being pig-headed."

"And you're being a dreamer. You've never groomed in your life."

Judy had been a professional groom for three years and knew the job inside out. But she was off sick. I was here, fit, enthusiastic and I knew Donavon like an old friend.

"At least give me a chance. At least go down putting up a fight. I've spoken to my parents and they're happy for me to go. I can stay in the grooms' dormitory and Camilla, her mother and

24

Zoe will all be there. Camilla's aunt lives just outside Burnley village."

Ash growled under his breath and kicked a bale flying down the heap. "Has anyone ever told you you're a bully?"

I was just about to volley back a perfect answer when an earth-shattering clatter of hoofs filled the yard. All our horses were tucked up in bed.

Wordlessly we shot out of the barn, hay seeds trickling down my neck, the bright evening sun dazzling as I screwed up my eyes and made a shield with my hand.

An enormous liver chestnut was stamping irritably at the ground, its rider pushing it forward circling on a tight rein. It was so powerful it looked more like a bull: every muscle was tautly defined, its belly and flanks were all scrunched up and it was swishing its tail with real venom. It must have been all of seventeen hands and part Hanoverian.

The rider was equally impressive; dark, moody, with a chest and arms like Hulk Hogan. He was the kind of rider you saw on posters in pony magazines.

Zoe was on the veranda outside the common room trying to rediscover her composure. She was completely bowled over and didn't seem to be able to function in any capacity. Her delicate freckled complexion was firing up like a furnace.

The rider eased back in the saddle giving the horse its head and sticking his legs out so it was impossible not to notice the rigid new cowboy boots and the flashy spurs.

Zoe was wittering nervously and pointing across in our direction. I suddenly became aware that Ash and I had come out of the barn at the same time looking ruffled, and started blushing to the roots of my hair.

Ash had frozen, almost grey with rage. The vibes sparking off him were electric with animosity. My initial interest was immediately doused and I just stood there wondering what on earth was going on.

"Hello, Jack." There wasn't a grain of friend-liness.

"Well if it isn't Ash the Flash, my old mate." The rider broke into a broad grin but the rest of his face was hard and there was an edge to his voice. "I see you're still pulling the babes – some things never change."

"What do you want?" Ash clenched both his fists, a muscle ticking furiously in his neck.

"That's not much of a welcome, Ashy-boy. And to think I've only been back three weeks." He gave a snide little laugh and let his eyes rove over my top and jeans just enough to make me feel uncomfortable.

"The States can have you." Ash curled up his

top lip in disgust. "I'd pay out for Concorde to see the last of you."

"From what I've heard, old boy, you couldn't even afford a bus fare."

Ash visibly stiffened. It was like something straight out of a novel. One was so blond and golden, the other dark and menacing, but both could set girls on edge with their startling good looks. I was reminded of two stallions locked in combat. For the life of me I couldn't work out who he was or why Ash hadn't mentioned him. He had the deep burnt-in tan of someone who'd spent a long time abroad and a distinctive American drawl. But he wasn't known on the British circuit.

With a cat-like telepathy he levelled his gaze straight at me, reading my thoughts. I winced with embarrassment and let my eyes slither away.

"Hasn't he told you where we first met?" He let the chestnut have his head and slung up a thigh to loosen the girth. His eyes were so dark and direct that they were like two black bullets. Despite the heat I started shivering all over, goose pimples popping up all along my arms.

"Hasn't he told you about the Youth Detention Centre?"

It was so much a bolt out of the blue I almost stumbled backwards.

Ash had turned a sickly yellow. He lunged

forward, grimacing, shaking, completely thrown. "Get out, Landers, before I knock you off that horse."

"Tut tut tut. Another Burgess secret. Another skeleton to cram in the cupboard. Now let me see, what else can I let out of the bag?"

Ash blasted forward, his fist balled tight. I grabbed his arm and clung on, fear thundering in my chest. "Leave it," I shrieked. "He's not worth it. He'll do you for assault."

"Good girl. Good advice. You know, you remind me so much of my groom. I think you've met her – Sasha. Very fanciable."

The hot sweaty late afternoon suddenly felt curiously dead. All I could hear was a wasp flitting around a hanging basket and a plane overhead. Two and two frantically clicked together in my mind but my body was a numb shell.

Right on cue, Donavon sprawled his huge head and neck over the door, trailing a streamer of hay and staring at the chestnut.

"Yes, that's right, Burgess, I'm after your horse. And when I get him I'm going to ride him into the ground. An eye for an eye. Remember. Is it all coming back?" There was real hatred in those black eyes now. "And just in case you're wondering about the money – here, get your peepers round that."

He yanked a newspaper from inside his shirt

and slung it down on the ground at Ash's feet. "I told you I'd be back. I promised you. And what goes up has to come down. You're finished, Ashy-boy. Kaput. You're history."

He wheeled the chestnut round so viciously its hocks nearly slid underneath it. Cockily he blew a kiss at Zoe who was still standing gaping and rode out of the yard without looking back.

I picked up the paper feeling repulsed, and flattened it out. The headline blared out. It was the Evening Recorder. The local paper. It carried today's date.

"Sir Charles adds eventing to his equine port-folio. His new protégé speaks out for the first time. Whiz-kid from the US, Jack Landers, aged 19, lands full sponsorship deal."

Even as I was reading out loud Ash was walking away. Towards Donavon's stable. He was walking away from the worst news possible. He was walking away from eventing.

CHAPTER FOUR

As it turned out, Donavon *was* going to Burnley. But only because the bank manager had insisted and threatened to pull the plug on Ash's finances if he didn't compete.

I was going to be groom and Judy had given me huge lists of instructions which I decided to pin up inside the horsebox so they wouldn't get lost. There was a hundred pound prize for best turned out horse and I was determined to win it.

Donavon was looking sensational but Ash didn't show the slightest interest. He schooled him for an hour in the afternoon and that was it. George and the novice horses had all been turned out. Ash seemed to have withdrawn from the sport he'd thrived on since the age of six. His heart wasn't in it any more. In fact his heart wasn't in anything. We hadn't been out on a date for over a week. We never mentioned Jack Landers.

Zoe received a bouquet of flowers signed "an admirer" and the initial J. I picked them up and flung them out of the window and Zoe refused to talk to me for two days.

I was getting up at the crack of dawn to give

Donavon an hour and a half of roadwork before school and then going back at four-thirty to ride Barney. Camilla said it was all beyond the call of duty and why didn't I find myself a new man, someone like Jasper Carrington who knew how to enjoy himself. I pretended to be sick and stepped up Donavon's grooming by another twenty minutes. Both my parents were on the warpath because I'd pinched my mum's favourite tea towel to use as a stable rubber and my dad's new car-cleaning sponge to wipe under the tail. Then I'd videoed a horse-carriage programme over an episode of Coronation Street.

By the grace of God neither Zoe nor I had posted the begging letter off to Sir Charles. All round the village, people were gossiping about the all-weather gallops which were being erected at Brooklands. Convoys of JCBs rattled along the lanes and sent the horses flying into the hedges. Ash just buried his head in the sand and once when I saw Jack out on exercise I dived over a small post and rail fence and shot off in the opposite direction.

The ground was rock hard and I was really worried about Donavon's legs. We called the blacksmith out to fit some special pads under his front shoes to act as shock absorbers. Camilla insisted on trying on a new white dress in front of the blacksmith which had him goggle-eyed, especially when she started fiddling with the zip at the front.

"I can't wait to get to Burnley. Think of all those gorgeous Australians, and with any luck you might get the stable next to William McNally-Smith."

Zoe, who'd been on edge for days, flew off to answer the telephone.

"Cam, do you ever think of anything other than men?" I raised my eyes heavenwards as she did another twirl and started wittering on about a particular New Zealander's bottom.

"That was Eric!" Zoe came out of the common room trying to disguise her obvious disappointment. "He says if you don't get down to the Pony Club in the next half hour, he's not going to be responsible for his actions."

All the Pony Club activities were held on the main county showground which had over two hundred ready-built stables and livestock barns which were ideal for dormitories during summer camp. Eric had been roped in to teach at a rally because one of the instructors was off with glandular fever. I'd promised to help and then completely forgotten when the blacksmith arrived unexpectedly.

As soon as I rode through the main gates

Barney seemed to grow six inches. He loved crowds of people, noise and any chance to show off. Most of the young pony clubbers were ardent members of his fan club and came racing up, all glassy-eyed and asking permission to stroke him. Zoe had nicknamed them "Barnettes" and one little girl with pigtails had asked if Barney had royal connections.

I pushed him into a trot and made my way over to a circle of cars, mainly four-wheel drives, where parents were scuffling around with fold-up chairs and thermos flasks. Eric's voice could be heard booming out from a cross-country fence sounding croaky and extremely rattled.

The scene was one of complete devastation. Half a dozen members on tiny ponies were paddling in a shallow area of water. One parent was up to her shins wading around trying to catch an over-fat Shetland who was plunging bottom-first like a hippo. Eric was over by a small bank lecturing a boy who looked as if he'd fallen off on his head.

"I've told you once, I've told you twice to lean back. Now if you want to carry on trying to kill yourself go ahead, but do it in your own time."

The boy promptly burst into tears and someone led up his pony who was fat and obviously ate too much rich grass. Eric put his head in his hands and didn't speak for a very long time.

"Oh Alex, how lovely to see you." Mrs Brayfield, the pony club secretary, bounced up, over-enthusiastic as ever. "As you can see, everything is totally under control."

"You're not putting enough work into him." Eric examined Barney like a show judge, wheeling his chair into all angles, his lips puckered up with disapproval.

All the parents had gone home leaving behind a debris of litter and one lone headscarf which was blowing up in the breeze. Barney gazed longingly at the cross-country fences and fidgeted irritably when I wouldn't let him have his head.

"You're spreading yourself all over the place." Eric thumped his arm down on the wheelchair which he often did when he was trying to make a point. "All this palaver over Burnley, charging around after Ash. Do you think Linford Christie dallies around helping everyone but himself? You're an athlete, Alex, and so is Barney. You've got to be single-minded."

He rooted around under his blanket and pulled out a sheet of paper which he handed up to me.

"A hundred sit-ups. Twenty press-ups. A hundred skips and a ten-minute jog. Daily. Two pints of full cream milk. Daily. Watch Mark Todd video. Daily. Eight hours sleep. Nightly."

"I can't do this," I screeched, looking down in horror at the scrawly writing. "I'm half dead with exhaustion as it is."

"Nonsense. At that last event you were puffing like a donkey. Barney carried you over the last half dozen fences. More stamina. More upper body strength. It's the only way."

"But . . ."

"No buts. You've got major competitions ahead. You're my pupil. I'm expecting a lot from you."

"You're doing this on purpose," I pouted, already deciding I wasn't doing the press-ups.

"I care, that's all. I want you to live up to your true potential. Not be a nearly-person who could always have done better. Is that clear?"

"Yes, sir." I saluted and then creased into a grin. There was no changing Eric. He was cantankerous and a slave-driver but if anyone could turn me into a champion it was him.

"Now, about this Jack Landers." I nearly fell off Barney head first myself. Last time I'd mentioned that name he'd gone off at the deep end.

"I want you to know what you're letting yourself in for. You realize he'll be at Burnley?"

I nodded, wondering what he was going to

say next. Eric gazed bleakly around as if searching for the right words.

"Jack was at boarding school in Yorkshire, with Ash, for five years. They were buddies, close, you know what I mean. Jack's parents weren't interested in him. Just kept palming him off on people – those types should never have kids in the first place. Jack had a horse, a real looker called Casino. Jack adored him, worshipped him – Casino became like his family. Anyway, one day when Jack had German measles Ash was exercising Casino on the moor. Ash came across a walker, a young girl who had fallen badly – she had a broken leg, I think. She was a diabetic, and needed her insulin. Ash had to get help and he was miles from the nearest house. He was only fifteen. He set Casino into a gallop and headed for the nearest road. Nobody knew Casino had a heart murmur – he collapsed and died instantly. Ash was lucky to be thrown clear. Jack never got over his death and blamed Ash. He said Ash had been overriding him. From that day on he became a changed lad, mean, aggressive, no compassion. Horses became just machines to him.

"Anyway, to cut a long story short, Jack set fire to the school and tried to frame Ash. Then he did the same with a couple of cars, and someone ended up in hospital. Ash got put in a detention centre. When Ash's innocence was finally proved,

Jack took off to America and to my knowledge only came back three weeks ago. He made a name for himself out there. He always was a cracking rider."

"You knew about Sir Charles sponsoring him, didn't you? He told you."

"Yes, I did. I've known for about six weeks."

"And you haven't said a word about all this?"

"No, it's none of my business. It was all a long time ago. Jack could be a changed person."

"But he isn't. He's a psychopath."

"He's disturbed, which is why I'm telling you all this. It's for your own good."

"Oh great." A prickle of cold fear lifted the hairs on the back of my neck. "I feel really safe now."

I could hardly believe what I'd just heard. I somehow felt like the victim, the piggy in the middle.

"You should have told me." I was utterly gutted. "Ash should have told me. And you should have told Sir Charles."

"I know." Eric glanced up, his eyes trailing away with guilt. "But it's too late now."

Back at the yard it was like a ghost town. There was a message pinned to Barney's stable door from Zoe saying she'd gone home early to finish a maths assignment. I know she'd got it into her head to be a horse physiotherapist but she'd never been that conscientious before.

Mum came to pick me up from the stables and we drove home through the town centre. There were queues of people outside the cinema waiting to see the latest blockbuster and I strained to catch a glimpse of what else was showing. Not that Ash ever had the time to take me.

There was a girl standing apart from the main crowd, her head down, dressed up to the hilt in black skirt and orange halter-neck top. She had a pretty face and short sandy hair but she looked so sad and empty. She'd obviously been stood up. I didn't have to look twice to recognize my best friend. It was Zoe standing outside the cinema. Waiting for a man.

CHAPTER FIVE

Dressage bridle, rolled reins, flash noseband, cross-country bridle, rubber reins . . . Brown and blue weight cloth, numnah, overreach boots, breastplate . . .

I'd never seen so much equipment and it all had to be crammed into battered metal trunks and packed away in the horsebox.

It was the morning of the big day and my stomach was tied in knots with a tantalizing mixture of nerves and excitement. I was grooming at one of the biggest three-day events in the country. I wasn't just a spectactor looking in, I would actually be there, rubbing shoulders with the famous, with a job to do, someone important. I vowed to take notes on how all the major riders warmed up their horses and then realized I didn't have a pen or paper. There were jackets and horse rugs strewn everywhere. I grabbed Judy's list, squinting with concentration, and tried to swallow down a sudden wave of panic.

Fairy liquid, grease, rubber gloves, cotton wool, bucket for equipment in ten-minute halt box, towels . . .

It was 6.30 a.m. and half the things still weren't packed.

Ash lowered the ramp, which creaked to the ground on huge springs, and I heard him rattling one of the hooks fitting up a hay net. Another crippling bout of nerves washed over me. Get a grip, Alex, get a grip . . .

Another of Judy's lists was taped to the cupboard door: "Check supplies – cornflakes, sugar, coffee, tea, skimmed milk, orange squash."

I fingered my little round cardboard "Groom's pass" and couldn't resist a self-indulgent smirk.

"Time to load up!" Ash banged the groom's door and went to lead out Donavon. Everything was in place, everything was running like clockwork.

Donavon bounded up the ramp in one stride, anxious to be getting off. Horses know when there is a special occasion, they can sense the excitement, the anticipation.

He was bandaged up in double gamgee, with travelling boots on top, and wore a tail guard attached to a surcingle with a sweat rug and travelling rug over the top. It had taken me ages to work out how to put the whole lot together.

Ash was just in jeans and an open-necked white shirt. All the top hat and tails and black jacket and jods were packed away in the horsebox wrapped in cling film.

Donavon was in, the partition in place, already tucking into his hay, his eyes bright as buttons as he looked out of the small plastic window. Ash ran back to the house to fetch his mobile phone and sunglasses and suddenly an idea hit me like midsummer madness, and I had just minutes to carry out my plan.

"I'm going to have a full English breakfast, mushrooms, tomatoes, crispy bacon, eggs."

"Don't forget the sausage and black pudding." Ash leaned across, clasping my hand in his, giving me one of his seductive, drop-dead gorgeous smiles. "Have I told you, Miss Johnson, that you've got the most beautiful pair of hands? It's just a shame about the face."

We'd been on the road about an hour and it was absolute bliss. The sun was well up now like a plump orange and we were making good time. All the signs ahead pointed to Services and I couldn't wait until I could uncross my legs and head for the nearest loo. I pulled off my sweatshirt and realized I'd got my T-shirt on inside out, so frantically got dressed again. Ash started singing and I didn't think I'd ever felt more happy.

We decided to pull into the garage first and fill up with diesel. It must have been the fumes which caused all the commotion.

Ash was just unscrewing the lid on the tank

and lifting up the nozzle. I was examining my face in the side mirror. The garage attendant was watching cynically as if we were going to take the roof off with us when we pulled out.

Suddenly the whole rear end of the box started to shake. It was like something in a horror movie. The reinforced metal sides quivered as pounding hoofs thundered in a barrage of manic kicks.

"Alex, help!" Ash replaced the nozzle. "He's gone off his head!"

The attendant raced out, terrified that he was going to have a loose horse tearing around the forecourt. Ash was yanking at the ramp, pulling out metal stops. Two teenagers ran forward, keen to help.

The ramp creaked down, bits of wood-shavings floating all over the place. Suddenly the crescendo of noise dulled to nothing. It just went deadly quiet.

Ash stared into the horsebox, turning grey with shock and disbelief. I stood trembling with my fingers crossed behind my back. Donavon smiled out at us, sweating gently but none the worse for wear.

But Ash's eyes weren't focused on Donavon – he was staring at the partition next door, the one that should have been empty. I closed my eyes trying to find suitable words but just felt my throat go bone dry.

"Alex." Ash's voice didn't even sound human.

Barney's big yellow head stared back at him, all lopey ears and cheeky grin. He looked like an errant schoolboy who had been caught red-handed in some stupid prank.

His face was a picture of contrite apology. "Sorry, Mum, but I was just feeling bored," is what he would have said if he could talk.

Ash didn't notice. He was leaning against the side of the box, his breathing coming in shallow sharp gasps. "Please somebody tell me this isn't happening."

"Is there a problem?" The garage attendant hastened across, obviously relieved that all the noise had subsided.

"Oh no, not a problem." Ash raked a hand through his hair, flipping it back, reflecting his desperation. "Not a problem." He glared at me and then Barney. "Just a thumping great disaster."

"I thought he would be company for Donavon." I was nervously pleating a duster in the front seat.

Ash was grinding the gears, threatening to pull the gearstick clean out of its socket.

"What inspired you to do such a thing? I can't understand." Despite his blistering anger he was actually trying.

"It's good experience for Barney – you know he loves travelling. You won't even know he's there, I promise. And Donavon will really appreciate his presence."

"Oh Alex, he's not some gormless bounding dog that you can keep on a lead, although I admit he behaves like one. Where is he going to stay?"

I gritted my teeth to stop my bottom lip trembling. "There's no need to shout."

"I'm not shouting." Ash raised his voice by ten decibels. "I'm merely speaking over you."

I stared out of the window determined to sulk. It was turning into a steaming hot day and I felt sticky and clammy.

"We'll be the laughing stock of the whole show. He's the worst behaved horse in the whole country."

We travelled on in silence. Twice I navigated badly and we had to do a ten-point turn in a narrow lane. Then we had to take a detour to avoid a low bridge. Neither of us had accounted for the six bales of hay strapped onto the roof rack.

When we finally got into the showground we had to wait ages while a vet checked Donavon's passport for vaccinations and identification. Luckily I had Barney's papers in the glove compartment from the last event.

Ash was frustrated by the delay and it was

46

even worse when we saw Jack Landers swaggering across one of the sanded pathways, a stockman's hat covering those menacing black eyes. He looked up, stopped, stared, allowed us a thin smile and then walked on.

"The twit," Ash hissed under his breath, his knuckles whitening as he gripped the steering wheel.

But I wasn't listening. I was utterly entranced by the sheer atmosphere and excitement of a major three-day event.

There were horses everywhere, grooms leading them out for grass, lunging quietly in corners. There was a professional buzz of anticipation but unlike small horse events everybody knew what they were doing. There were no mishaps. Nobody falling off or saddles slipping under hairy fat bellies. Everybody was organized.

Ash headed towards the parking area and the stables came into view. Rows of temporary wooden installations with numbers on every door. I did a quick double-take when I thought I saw Christy Mitchell coming back from a hot dog stall and then I saw a foreign rider who looked just like Keanu Reeves gabbling away to his trainer and sitting on a fabulous bay mare who reminded me of George.

"If your eyes get any bigger, they'll fall out of their sockets." Ash glanced across at me with a

47

smidgen of warmth in his voice. He was finally thawing, which was a good job because Barney needed a stable, food, hay and woodshavings and it was all going to cost.

Donavon came out of the box a little stiff but perfectly OK. He took everything in his stride and waited patiently as Ash peeled off his boots. Barney thundered down the ramp, over-eager and enthusiastic, nearly falling straight on his nose and dragging me over to a stable marked "152" where a chestnut mare shot back from her door looking petrified. Barney whickered a greeting and looked wounded when she showed him her teeth. Ash cast his eyes heavenwards in despair.

"For goodness' sake, Alex, that's Maggie Weston's horse. Get him away from there! And can you try and keep his romantic urges under control. He's worse than Jasper Carrington."

Donavon was soon settled in his stable marked "192" and I left Barney tied up outside while I shuffled up the woodshavings and wiped off his coat, putting the body brush through his mane and tail. Any minute now I'd have to start plaiting up for the veterinary inspection. This was a very official affair and the horses had to be immaculate. This was where the "best turned out" was being judged, but looking round at the incredible standard my hopes sagged like a deflated soufflé. I didn't stand a chance.

Ash liked as many plaits as possible, between 18 and 22, which he said showed off Donavon's beautiful powerful neck. I had all the instructions, written down by Judy, which I stuck on the wall with some Blu-Tack. Donavon stood like a rock while I divided his mane into bunches and threaded the thick black cotton. By the time Ash came back from trying to find a stable for Barney I was a good third of the way down his neck and feeling competent. I was even starting to enjoy myself. The inspection was at 3.50 which left me a good two and a half hours to get ready.

Ash opened the stable door looking in far better spirits and clutching a glass of champagne and a tiny box of strawberries which he said cost £4.50. He'd found a stable for Barney right at the end of the line which was a bit cramped but at least it would keep him quiet.

Very gently he popped a strawberry in my mouth and gave me a tantalizing kiss. I was just starting to tingle all over and wrap my arms round his gorgeous tanned neck when he pulled back, suddenly concerned.

"I think you ought to go and get Barney out of the horsebox now before he gets into trouble. Somehow I won't be happy until he's bolted in."

I stood back, letting my arms slip round his waist, smiling reassuringly, feeling on cloud nine.

"Don't be silly," I said. "He's tied up outside. There's nothing to worry about."

Ash stiffened, his eyes darkening to new depths. "He's not, Alex. He's not there."

"Of course he is, he's right over there . . ."

The head collar hung limp from the lead rope, the buckle torn off and the main headpiece ripped in half. Right at the other end of the showground we suddenly heard a sharp, shrill, blood-curdling scream.

I knew it was Barney. It was as if I'd developed a sixth sense. Ash quickly put down the strawberries on an upturned bucket and grabbed my hand. Whatever that scream was in aid of, Barney had something to do with it. He was right in the thick of it. We both knew it. Right up to his stubby black hocks.

CHAPTER SIX

"Barney!" I yelled, as we arrived gasping at a medium-sized enclosure which was already thronging with people. It was the Children's Farm and I could already see Barney strutting around gleefully, a sheep on one side and a cockerel wafting around on the other.

A woman in a voluminous sun hat was still screeching, examining her young son who apparently had "a big double-topper ice cream snatched from his little hands by that ugly old camel. It's a wonder he's still alive."

An official tried to console her while Ash went to buy a new ice cream and I sneaked into the farmyard, intent on grabbing Barney and then disappearing in a puff of smoke. I had to pinch a head collar from an obliging donkey and then drag him out through a tiny yellow gate. To make matters worse, I slid in some sheep muck and twisted my arm.

Ash insisted on witnessing Barney being locked in his new stable which was only about ten by eight and full of cobwebs. Barney pulled a face like a child being left at a new school. I put a clip on the bolt of the door so that he couldn't nuzzle it straight out and Ash propped up a plank of wood under the hinge which I thought was a teeny bit excessive.

Back in Donavon's stable the plaits I'd done were all still in place and so were the strawberries. I stuffed my face and then set about plait number nine. Ash went to get changed in the horsebox and somebody turned up a tape of *Phantom of the Opera* in the next stable which I found quite soothing. Maybe that was the idea. All animals were said to respond to music, having their certain preferences. Barney, who had terrible taste, had always favoured Rod Stewart.

The vet's inspection was to be held on the drive outside the house, which was more like a stately home. A section of gravel had been swept back to reveal smooth level tarmac which would show whether a horse was totally sound. The slightest hint of any lameness and that was it – out. Never mind all that training and months of preparation. The horse came first.

It was a real art trotting up a horse properly and Ash had asked me to put on Donavon's bridle for extra control. Across the aisle in the other stables there were a lot of vaguely familiar faces. A rider in the tightest white jodhpurs I'd ever seen was chatting up his groom, who was more interested in reading the *Daily Mirror*. She stuffed a sleeping bag in his arms and told him to go and calm down in the horsebox. "Ah, can't I decide what bag I sleep with?" he replied.

She pulled a face and started chatting to a girl groom with dramatic white streaks who was moaning that she wasn't going to the Olympics.

The inspection was underway, the loud-speaker calling up each horse. A jolt of apprehension flickered through my entire body and I grabbed the tail gloss and set to work.

"You look stunning!"

Ash had raced back to the stables in a dark blazer, trousers, white shirt and stripy tie. I hadn't realized it would be such a dressed-up affair.

"Quick, there's no time to lose." He was carrying a lunge rein, cavesson and lunge whip and he looked in no mood for arguing. "They're pulling horses out who look even remotely stiff. I don't want to take any chances."

"But Ash, I've only just got him ready!"

"Tough." He flashed me a boyish grin. "Welcome to the world of eventing."

We found a quiet corner over by some chestnut trees where the ground was level. It seemed everybody was having the same idea at the same time. There were horses being lunged everywhere.

Donavon went beautifully. Ash stood on the perimeter watching with eagle eyes as I let him circle round me on the end of the rein. I felt like a total professional, flicking him on with the whip, making him track up, tweaking the rein ever so gently so he bent his nose in the right direction. Ash gave me the thumbs up and a smile of pure honey. I was back in his good books, I was doing everything right. Then I took my eyes off Donavon for a split second and my euphoria crumbled like a stack of cards.

Somehow the lunge rein had become entangled round his forelegs and instead of staying calm, panic shot straight through me and down the rein to Donavon. I was nearly dragged off my feet and then Donavon stumbled, pecked and went down on his nose.

Ash froze with horror. Donavon plunged, bucketed and then stood trembling, his eyes rolling in alarm. A clutch of bystanders ran across, everybody desperately tense. A jockey-sized groom with a ponytail grabbed Donavon's reins and pulled him forward and I could do nothing but close my eyes.

"He's sound, just a bit shaken, but he'll live."

"Oh Lord." I leaned on Donavon's shoulder watching the familiar green Fiesta bounce over the field at about ten miles an hour. A parking attendant waved frantically but Eric shot to the left and completely ignored him. He was heading straight for us.

"Oh no." Ash followed my gaze, his face

crinkling in amazement. "Someone tell me this isn't happening."

Eric hardly ever went to horse events. And never when Ash was competing. That was the agreement. The two of them clashed like bulls and had completely differing ideas on training. So if that was the case, what was Eric doing here now?

As he approached, Eric wound the window down, amazingly relaxed and chirpy. But it was the occupant of the passenger seat who really had me gawping.

The imposing man swept out of the car. He was wearing a heavy reddish-brown tweed suit which matched his thick coarse reddish thatch of hair.

Ash looked stunned.

"Hello, Sir Charles." Ash looked him straight in the eye. Only I could see the nerve flicking madly in his neck. "You never told me you were acquainted." He glared at Eric.

"My dear boy." Eric was savouring every minute. "You never asked. We have both been invited to stay at the house by Sir James Burnley."

"Number 62!" A steel grey throughbred shot forward, dragging a young girl who looked terrified.

I knew just how she felt. Donavon was standing quietly, watching, as good as gold, which at least was something. Ash methodically picked imaginary dirt out of his fingernails and fiddled with the buckles on Donavon's bridle.

The girl with the white streaks was gossiping away behind me holding on to a pleasant-looking bay and discussing snogging. "Well at least you're having more luck than me. The most I've pulled lately is a muscle."

Someone else was nattering on about recipes and what could be done with cabbage when suddenly I caught a glimpse of Sasha Fennington pushing through the crowds. She was wearing dark sunglasses and even from a distance it was obvious she was upset. Jack Landers barged after her, leading the massive chestnut we'd seen in the yard, his pale skin flaming up with temper. "You can't leave now. You're supposed to be my groom, you scatty cow."

Sasha ignored him, thrust a lead rope in his hands and ran off in the direction of the stables.

"She's weird," the girl with the white streaks whispered too loudly behind me. "There's something seriously wrong with that girl, mark my words."

"We're on!" Ash suddenly grabbed Donavon's reins, ripping off his front protector boots and leading him forward. "Alex, will you pull yourself together. You look as if you've seen a ghost."

Donavon passed his inspection. Four horses

in all were pulled out before the first day's competition. Everything was now focused on the dressage at 11.40 the next morning.

We didn't win the best turned out. My plaits weren't good enough and Donavon had still got the remnants of a dirt stain on his nose from where he'd fallen. Jack Landers swaggered over to pick up the £100 first prize on behalf of Sasha. The girl with the white streaks offered to lead the chestnut back to the stables and flirted outrageously at every opportunity. Jack patted her bottom and gave her a couple of notes from Sasha's envelope. The creep.

I gave Donavon a hay net and light tea and took out his plaits as soon as possible so that the hairs wouldn't break down. Barney gobbled up everything in sight and Ash had to chuck down another bale of hay from on top of the horsebox.

I never realized grooming at a three-day event would be such hard work. I never seemed to have a moment's rest. Ash went off to walk the cross-country course while I tidied the horsebox and was convinced I caught a glimpse of Ian Jones floating around the stables in a pair of Union Jack shorts.

Eric came round at about six o'clock with a bag bursting with cream cakes and insisting I use a teapot instead of throwing a teabag in a mug and beating the life out of it. The only way we could get his wheelchair in was for me to drag him up the ramp, through the horse partitions and into the living quarters.

I was begging him to help Ash with the cross-country. "You've got to advise him." I perched on the formica table which was piled up with horse rugs. "His mind isn't on the job. And I feel responsible. What if he breaks his neck or something? I couldn't bear it."

"Typical Alex, as subtle as a sledgehammer." Eric looked in the cupboard for a milk jug. "Ash will take care of himself. He's a big boy now – he doesn't need his old crippled uncle sticking his beak in where it's not wanted. He'll give Donavon the ride of his life because it's his last performance and he's got something to prove."

"Well, you've got more faith than me." I stumped over to the mini fridge. "At the moment Ash Burgess is dragging himself around like a jellyfish."

"The Chocolate Bar" was in a disused barn with straw bales to sit on interspersed with the odd plastic seat. There was music playing and drinks available, anything from coke in a pint plastic cup to gin and tonic and whisky and soda.

Ash finally decided to take me at nine o'clock at night when it was packed like a sardine tin. Everybody was talking about the Farmyard Complex which was a new fence on the cross-country course and just about unjumpable. The problem was the fence out which was massive and had no ground line. Horses always jump better if a fence is solid and filled in and has a definite take-off point. This had neither and, even worse, was in the direction of a small wood. Horses hate jumping into darkness. Three riders sitting in a corner were frantically drawing diagrams on white paper napkins.

Someone came up and shook Ash's hand up and down like mad, and then gave me a kiss on the cheek. The light was dim which was probably a good thing as I definitely looked the youngest by at least five years.

"I hear your horse is up for sale?" A thick-set man with buck teeth pushed his way across towards the bar. I kept my eyes lowered and tried to avoid his octopus hands which were intent on snaking round my waist.

"Hands off! She's far too good for you." Jack Landers padded up behind me like a dangerous big cat, winking cheekily and thrusting a drink in my hand.

Ash froze as soon as he saw him. Sasha was over by the bar looking pale and washed out and ordering more drinks. I knew I shouldn't have insisted that Ash come here. It was a stupid thing to do.

Jack kept on smiling. There was no doubt he

was ultra-sexy. I despised him but, despite myself, I felt irresistibly drawn to those black burning eyes and that cruel mouth.

"Just for once, Ash, let's bury the hatchet. Let's have a drink for old times' sake, eh? Or have you turned tee-boring-old-total?"

One of Jack's mates, a well-spoken tall guy called Julian, passed over two cocktails with cherries floating in the middle.

"We call these Farmyard Complexes." Jack leaned back and started laughing demonically at his own joke. "They are what you call extremely dangerous." His eyes fell on me as if he was trying to send me a special message. "But of course your girlfriend is far too young for one of those." He was getting drunker by the minute.

Sasha looked as if she was going to burst into tears and hovered in a corner casting her eyes endlessly towards the door. Amazingly Ash accepted the drink and downed it in one. "Tomorrow I'm going to thrash you, Jack Landers."

Suddenly a big Australian pushed in, splitting up the group and splintering the tension. I grabbed Ash by the arm and dragged him towards the door.

"I'll have the next one on Casino, shall I?" Jack's voice was taunting. "Poor dead Casino." But Ash didn't rise to the bait.

For a second I thought Sasha made a move to try and stop me, to say something. Then her eyes glassed over with uncertainty and she pushed her way to the ladies' loos. She was a different person from the one who'd turned up to try out Donavon. She was scared, nervy, on edge. She was carrying some great dark secret around.

But if somebody had told me the truth there and then I wouldn't have believed them.

CHAPTER SEVEN

The noise was unmistakable. The soft patter of footsteps right outside the grooms' dormitory. I leant across and peered at my watch. 2.15 in the morning. Whoever was trudging around out there wasn't just looking at the stars. I grabbed the torch from the bedside and pulled on an anorak.

The door clicked open and I stumbled out into the warm sticky night. I took Ash's cross-country whip for some kind of protection but didn't think it would be much use. The grass was dry and prickly under my bare feet. And I had to stop and wait a few seconds while my eyes adjusted to the darkness. Some clouds moved across the darkened sky revealing a full moon, which suddenly lit up the whole of the stable complex in a flood of soft light. And there was a darkened figure, bent over, creeping down the edge of the long line of boxes, towards Barney's stable.

My heart missed a beat. I was overcome by sheer panic. Barney was in that stable, all alone, vulnerable, with a potential horse attacker creeping towards him.

I tiptoed forward, keeping well up against the

side of the stables, horses rustling sleepily inside, the odd one poking its head over the door and nearly giving me a heart attack. Then I stubbed my toe on a feed bucket and had to bite my tongue to keep quiet.

The moon disappeared behind a barrier of cloud and I switched on the torch, hands trembling with fear. I heard a stable door open. I couldn't see a thing. Then I heard a faint whicker from a horse. It wasn't Barney. I'd recognize Barney's voice anywhere.

I crept round the edge of a pile of wood-shaving bales and then made a run for it towards the end of the row. The pale lemony light of my torch flickered on Barney's stable. Nothing. The door was shut and I couldn't see anything. But two doors down, a light was switched on. Both halves of the door were shut up but the light was flooding out from underneath. I didn't know whose horses were stabled there. I hadn't had chance to look. What if it was someone famous?

I crept further along, my heart sounding like a full-scale orchestra. Suddenly a horse snorted and I dropped the torch on my foot and yelped. Barney bulldozed his shoulders into the door, neighing in delight. The little sweetheart had recognized my voice. But this was no time to be making a scene.

The closed stable door clicked open and

somebody crept out carrying a bottle and a cloth which reminded me of chloroform in Agatha Christie movies. What if they were going to knock me out? The figure stood very still as I pressed painfully against the rough wood of Barney's door.

The moon reappeared, almost winking in the dark night. Then the figure turned looking petrified in my direction. I wondered if it was a horse rustler. Then I saw a familiar face. The familiar scared features, nervy, on edge. Sasha Fennington took one last look around and slid back in the stable. All I knew for certain was that it wasn't Jack Landers' stable. There was only one conclusion – Sasha Fennington was sabotaging a horse . . .

I'd have to burst into the stable. I could over-power her easily. She wasn't that big and I'd be catching her unwares. Flashing headlines flickered in my mind: "Teenage Groom Tackles Horse Doper."

Very carefully, very slowly, I got my fingers behind the top half door and took a very deep, very nervous breath. I'd have to catch her red-handed. After ten, no, after five. One. Two. Three. My breath started to rattle. Four. I tightened my closed fist round Ash's black plastic whip. *Five!*

The whole door flung back on its hinges. Sud-denly there seemed to be a blinding flash of fluorescent light, grey startled hindquarters and a scuffed cloud of salmon-pink shavings flying up all over.

Sasha just stood and stared, trembling. The dark woolly hat was pulled over her ears, emphasizing her wan little face and huge Bambi eyes which were filling with terror.

A remarkable grey horse lunged up the side of the walls, going mad with panic, its eyes rolling and its forelegs scrabbling. It was completely demented.

"Dolly, please calm down, it's OK." Sasha expertly went over to her, stroking the slender swan-like neck, checking the mad pawing, reassuring in such a way that the horse quickly calmed down and stood quaking, exhausted with the sudden panic.

"I might have known it'd be you." Sasha was annoyed but seemed in a strange way relieved. "Now you're here, come in and close the door and keep your voice to a whisper."

She picked up the cloth again and moved round to the horse's other side.

I was completely bowled over by the grey mare. Now she was standing quietly I could fully appreciate her beauty. She had the most incredible conformation, a classic head, wonderful shoulders, girth, strong but elegant clean legs and her hindquarters, the engine-house of any competition horse, were sensational. She looked unusual and ethereal because she was a delicate flea-bitten grey. This is when the grey hairs are smattered with little areas of black to give a speckled look. She reminded me of a delicate thrush's egg which could shatter at any moment. Her eyes still rolled wildly as soon as I made a movement. But she was a champion – it screamed out from every pore of her body. This delicate 15.3 hands mare could win a gold medal at the Olympics. She was class, she was a superstar.

"Who does she belong to?" All thoughts of drugs seemed to have disappeared from my mind. All I could wonder was why nobody had seen her at the inspection, why she was locked away in the second-best stables at the end of the line next to Barney.

"Sir Charles. She was a polo pony brought over from Argentina but she never really took to it. Apparently she was terrified of the polo sticks, and if you ask me someone gave her a good beating when she was young. You've had a tough life, haven't you, darling?"

"So why isn't she next to Jack's other horse and what are you doing out here at this time?"

The questions were hanging in the air, demanding answers.

Sasha didn't speak. She put down the yellow cloth, rubbed her hands on her trousers and gently placed a flat palm on the mare's flanks. Very carefully, clicking her tongue, she eased her over, stepping one hindleg across the other, until I could see the other side.

"There, does that answer your question?"

I drew in a sharp breath. Horror and outrage bit into my throat. "How, w-why? Who would do such a thing?"

The ugly red weeping weal marks were in regular stripes across her rump. They were ugly and deep, and quite frankly I didn't know how to handle it. How could somebody whip a horse like this? I couldn't comprehend it.

Sasha dabbed at a trickle of watery blood oozing out of one of the deeper cuts and Dolly leapt against the wall, quivering and sweating with pain and fear.

"You've got to get a vet," I croaked. "She may even need stitches. For goodness' sake, Sasha, I've never seen anything like it."

"No, no way. It's none of your business. She'll be all right."

"It was Jack, wasn't it? He did this. Why are you protecting him, Sasha? He's a scumbag. Why?"

"You don't understand. Nobody does. He's not that bad, really. He brought Dolly here to compete but she played up badly this morning in training – he's never gone this far before."

"Sasha!"

"You mustn't tell." She was openly pleading

68

now, her eyes huge. "For Dolly's sake, honestly, this is the best way."

"She needs medical attention."

"If it all comes out Sir Charles will get rid of her. He gave her to Jack because nobody could do anything with her. If she doesn't prove herself, she'll go to the sales. She'll end up being sold for meat."

Sasha turned and buried her head in Dolly's silky mane. "You've got to keep quiet, Alex, you've got to."

We spent the next hour bathing Dolly's wounds with warm water and TCP and I fetched some antiseptic powder from Barney's stable which we spent ages puffing on to her raw skin. We both agreed we couldn't possibly put on her rug just yet although I was panicking that if any flies got near, it could become infected.

We took her for a walk, mainly as a leg-stretch and for a bite of grass. The poor little love was as good as gold and breathed in the night air, glad to be out of her stable.

"Are you sure you'll be able to keep her out of sight tomorrow?"

Sasha gave Dolly an extra length of rope and seemed to be happier now she had someone to share the burden with. "Everybody will be focused on the dressage. And nobody comes down this end. I don't see a problem."

69

I picked a handful of grass for Barney who was straining over his door wondering what I was doing plodding around in pyjamas and an anorak at three o'clock in the morning. Dawn would soon be breaking and by six o'clock the stables would be a hive of activity.

Sasha explained how she'd worked for Jack in America, which had been a fantastic experience, but how she had no qualifications and Jack had threatened that if she left him he wouldn't give her a reference and he'd make sure she never worked with horses again.

"I was brought up in a high-rise flat in the East End of London. I never saw gardens. We had rising damp and cockroaches in the bedroom. I couldn't go back to that."

"But you wouldn't have to," I urged. "Jack's all mouth and trousers. He's a bully. You're brilliant with horses – you'd get another job."

We put Dolly back in the stable and cleared away all the wads of cotton wool. She looked much happier although we both hated having to close the top door. "We may have to put a rug on her tomorrow," I said, "in case anyone gets curious and looks in."

"Jack's not that bad, you know." Sasha caught my arm. "He's insecure, and he acts tough and hard as a defence."

"Don't try to convert me." I picked up the

70

antiseptic powder and gave Dolly one more friendly pat. "I'm going along with this for her sake, not Jack's. As far as I'm concerned Jack Landers is a pig."

Sasha visibly winced. "Just give me twenty-four hours. After that you can tell whoever you want."

"Just tell me one thing now." I gave her a direct, level gaze so she couldn't wriggle out of telling the truth. "Why do you protect Jack so much?"

Sasha stepped back, almost in surprise, her eyes widening but for once not filled with anxiety. "Oh, I'd have thought that was obvious." She smiled very delicately and for the first time I noticed just how pretty she was. "I love him."

CHAPTER EIGHT

"He's fantastic." Camilla and Zoe were strutting their stuff at nine o'clock the next morning, chatting up all the good-looking riders and pretending they were guest teen reporters from the pony magazine *In The Saddle*. They'd even managed to get into the strawberries and champagne tent free and had found a clipboard from somewhere. Camilla's leading question was "What do you eat for breakfast?"

"I'm sure you could think of something more spicy than that," I said with a solemn face. I was concentrating madly on Donavon. I was supposed to be walking him around to get him used to all the sights and sounds of the dressage arena. There were horses everywhere and the warm-up area was like Piccadilly Circus. Ash had gone back to the horsebox to get changed into his top hat and tails. I'd literally had to throw a jug of cold water over him to get him out of bed. There was a note under the windscreen wiper of the horsebox saying "Rise And Shine Sleeping Beauty". It was signed Jack. He'd put a sedative in Ash's drink last night.

Sasha caught my eye from across the arena.

She was leading Jack's huge liver chestnut aptly named The Terminator. We'd taken it in turns to check on Dolly, finally deciding to cover her hindquarters with a light cotton sheet and open the top half door. To anyone walking past she was just another horse withdrawn from the competition. Everybody was too wrapped up in their own affairs to care.

"Keep him on the move, Alex, and don't be intimidated." Eric suddenly appeared at the ringside looking particularly dapper in a panama hat. He winked at me and then I saw Ash walking past a hot dog stall looking absolutely gorgeous in a top hat and tails. My heart flipped over and I gave a huge sigh. For the millionth time I wondered how I'd been so lucky to find such a wonderful boyfriend. Ash had been voted Sexiest Hunk of the Year by *In The Saddle* and Most Promising Up-and-Coming Eventer. A tribe of young fans ran after him eagerly holding out pens and autograph books . . .

Camilla, who was strutting round in skintight jods, ran over to me all agog to announce she'd just spotted the showjumper Blake Kildaire in the VIP tent and she was going to angle for a date. The only trouble was he had a pretty young girl with him who looked too nice for words – but since when had that ever held her back?

Jack came out of the beer tent looking charismatic and as soon as he caught sight of Zoe hovering by the entrance he pinched a bunch of flowers from a special display and gave her a kiss on the cheek.

I gritted my teeth and felt a flutter of panic. Was my best friend falling for this moron? Was he the one she'd been waiting for anxiously outside the cinema? Every time I tried to ask her she clammed up and changed the subject. Sasha looked desolate from across the arena.

At 11.15, Ash waved me over and I tightened Donavon's girth ready for him to mount. The dressage judges were being particularly harsh and even some of the top international riders had been marked down heavily. Luckily their top number one rides were being saved for the Olympics.

Ash moved off, flexing Donavon from side to side, warming him up for the second time that day. Eric had taught me how important it was to stretch a horse's muscles properly before any serious work. Horses were just like athletes and needed the same care.

I saw Eric pursing his lips, dying to give advice but fighting it back, determined not to make any waves. Ash still looked groggy, even after half a dozen cups of treacle-black coffee.

Jack leered at him and vaulted onto The Terminator who pinned back his ears and gave an angry squeal.

"Come on, Donavon. Get into gear, Ash." Camilla was proving an embarrassment.

I quickly whisked over Donavon's quarters with a stable rubber while Ash was waiting to enter the arena. They both looked fantastic. Ash reminded me of the delicious Darcy in *Pride and Prejudice* and I vowed I must take a photograph before he got changed.

"More inside rein." Eric couldn't help himself as Ash walked majestically into the white-bordered enclosure.

This was it, seven minutes of total concentration: make or break time. Ash looked stony faced as he saluted the judges. Donavon had been known to boil over with excitement on important occasions. But this time he was listening to Ash's every command. Even the poker-faced judge with a sweet in his mouth seemed to be enjoying the performance. Ash crossed the diagonal in extended trot.

"He's made a right pig's ear of that." Eric was on tenterhooks. It looked perfect to me.

What next? A right half pass followed by collected canter. I knew the test off by heart. Donavon was really buckling down and producing the goods. What a star. People were really starting to take notice.

"Good lad." Eric clenched his fist. I didn't know who he was referring to, Ash or Donavon.

He rode out of the arena on a long rein looking absolutely chuffed.

"Not bad." Eric controlled his excitement with a totally sober look. I plastered Donavon's nose with kisses, and dropped sliced apples all over the place.

"I think you're in the top ten." Camilla was straining her neck. I crossed everything but my toes and my eyebrows. We had to do well.

Jack rode into the arena next, looking powerful and in charge. The Terminator didn't look so happy, swishing his tail and rolling his eyes but unable to get away from Jack's vice-like legs.

The electronic scoreboard flashed up the marks. Ash scored 48.8.

"That's brilliant," I screeched. "You're in second place."

"It's not over yet." Ash kept his feet on the ground.

"It is now," Camilla shrieked as The Terminator broke into canter at the wrong place. Unfortunately the rest of his test was brilliant and his marks would still be high.

Two competitors came up and shook Ash's hand and then a steward edged over to me, deeply embarrassed and seeming to want to disappear under his bowler hat. "Excuse me, are you Alexandra Johnson?" I nodded dumbly and fiddled with Donavon's reins.

"There's a funny little horse causing mayhem over in the sponsor's tent. The thing is nobody can do a thing with him and I've been informed you might be the owner." He gave me a wilting please-help smile and I felt as if I'd swallowed a jug of ice cubes. I came out in goose pimples. Oh Barney, what are you up to now?

I dived over a sagging rope and sprinted over to the stately tent, my heart throbbing in wild panic.

"Wait!" Sasha was suddenly behind me carrying a feed bucket and lead rope. "I thought you might need some help. He sounds a handful."

"To say the least," I gasped, wondering what I'd done in a former life to deserve such anxiety.

As soon as I entered the sponsor's tent I had to bite back tears. Three trestle tables had been knocked over and plates full of delicate sandwiches littered the grass floor.

Sir Charles came in behind me blocking off the daylight, looking daunting in a white suit.

"Well, don't just stand there." A lady with a squeaky voice and hair that looked like an advert for shampoo waved frantically towards the rear exit. "He went that way. Go and catch the brute before he comes back."

With a lurching heart I realized that Barney had made for the showjumping ring which was all set out for Sunday's performance.

The showjumps looked vast and impressive and there, leaping round the red brick wall like a little Bambi, was Barney. His face was almost clownlike with enjoyment. Two men in bowler hats were chasing after him, sweating profusely and cursing enough to turn the air blue. Oh Barney, please, enough is enough.

Sasha ran forward, rattling some horse nuts, and Barney's ears pricked forward and then his custard-yellow face clouded over with a knowing look. *You're not catching me that way.* I went one way and Sasha the other, with the hope of closing him in.

"Steady, boy, steady." I fixed him with a steady slow stare and very stubbornly, very rebelliously, he backed into a shallow open ditch.

"Barney!" Water sprayed up in a huge arc and then he had the gall to curl up his top lip and blow stupid watery bubbles at me. "That's it, Barney, I'm coming in."

My cheeks were burning with embarrassment. Sasha threw me a head collar and Barney immediately stuck his neck skywards so it was like trying to bridle a giraffe. In the end I had to vault onto his back and ride him out of the ditch where he left huge craters in the turf with his scrabbling hoofs.

The main entrance to the arena was padlocked with a tractor blocking the way so I had to ride him back through the marquee. It was the worst feeling in the world. The lady with the squeaky voice was mopping up egg mayonnaise sandwiches and Sir Charles was standing by the trestle tables armed with a camera which he promptly clicked so the flashlight went off in our faces.

"Funniest thing that's happened in years." He rewound the film.

By the time we got back to the dressage arena we had become celebrities.

Jack was waiting by the ropes, holding on to The Terminator who was shuffling nervously and straining against Jack's iron grip on his double bridle.

"Where the hell do you think you've been?" He flashed a look of white-hot fury at Sasha who started quaking in her boots. "I've been standing here like an idiot waiting for you. I'm dying of thirst and this idiot of a horse won't stand still."

"Maybe he's thirsty too." I glared at Jack and slipped down from Barney's back, ready to lead him to the stables.

"You keep out of it."

"It's true, Jack. You could have taken off his saddle and watered him." Sasha blurted out the words and then stood gaping, unable to believe what she'd just said.

Jack was speechless. He thrust the reins into

her hands and marched off. "I'll deal with you later."

The words were laden with threat and I couldn't help thinking how he'd sorted out poor Dolly.

"You can't let him treat you like that," I protested as soon as he was out of earshot. "The guy's an ape."

Sasha glanced away, her eyes filling with tears.

"We can't keep Dolly a secret, it's too serious." I made up my mind with concrete determination. "I'm going to put Barney in his stable, bolt the door and then I'm going to find Eric. He'll sort it out, he'll report Jack and he'll find you another job. You can trust him."

"No, please, Alex. You can't." Sasha ran after me, panic-stricken, her voice yammering, her shoulders shaking. "Please, Alex, don't!"

I didn't mean to knock her off balance. I whipped round too quickly when she clutched hold of my shirt sleeve. Somehow my leg tangled with hers and knocked her right off her feet. She fell to the ground, stretching out her left arm to take the brunt of the fall.

"Sasha!"

Thank God nobody was passing at the time. Everybody was up by the dressage arenas or by the main entrance.

The milky white hypodermic syringe rolled

out of her jeans pocket onto the dried shrivelled grass and lay there glinting in the sun like a terrible piece of evidence.

I'd never been so surprised in my entire life. I didn't know how to react.

"It's not what you think." Sasha leapt up, grabbing the syringe and stuffing it back in her pocket. "I don't do drugs."

"Oh no? So you just carry that around for effect, do you? Some fancy new way of taking vitamins?" I couldn't keep the sarcasm out of my voice. I felt cheated and dirty and somehow hurt that she hadn't told me the whole truth.

"I'm a diabetic."

It came out as a hard, cold fact of life and slapped me straight between the eyes. "I have been since I was thirteen years old."

"Oh."

"And I have a six-inch metal pin in my right leg where I broke it when I was fifteen. That's when I met Jack. He came to visit me in hospital."

"Oh." I was reeling now. Eric's words flooded back in great suffocating waves. Sasha was the girl on the moor.

"Alex, are you all right? You look weird."

I leant against Barney's neck, and closed my eyes. "So you saw Ash riding Casino?" I said eventually. "You heard about how he died?"

"It was an accident." Sasha dusted herself

82

down and tried to sound normal. "Jack wanted someone to blame and Ash fitted the bill. I never told Jack that I'd seen Casino die, that it wasn't Ash's fault. If I had he would have blamed me."

"Oh Sasha, what have you done?" I stared at her in disbelief. "All that vengeance all those years."

"That's why I feel so sorry for Jack now – Casino was the only one who loved him. He's so messed up, Alex. He needs help."

"That's no reason to treat you like dirt and use a beautiful innocent horse as a punch bag. I'm telling Eric, Sasha. Someone's got to sort out this whole sorry mess."

"No, Alex, please. Just give me another twenty-four hours."

Barney trotted back to his stable like a runaway tank obviously bored with the whole conversation.

The sun was burning now, I could feel the delicate skin on my shoulders starting to prickle. I was tired and I'd had no breakfast and I felt as if I was carrying a ten-ton weight on my shoulders.

Dolly stuck her pretty sensitive head out when she heard us approaching and then shot back, screaming with fear, crashing towards the rear of the stable.

Sasha ran forward.

Jack Landers was planted outside, his tough

muscular bulk blocking Barney's door. My stomach curdled just at the sight of him.

He had his head bent and his arms locked around a shapely female body. At first I thought it was the girl with the white streaks and then I remembered she'd been taken off to hospital with a broken toe. Jack Landers was snogging as if he was going for a new world record.

"Jack!" Sasha's voice cracked with emotion. She seemed disorientated.

Jack looked up, casually pushing the girl away but totally unfazed, as if he'd been caught watching television when he should have been washing the pots. His full pouting lips were gently smeared with pinky-orange lipstick.

"Zoe!" It was my turn to be shocked. Zoe Jackson, my best friend, was standing looking besotted and in the arms of the biggest louse in the area. And even worse, I hadn't known a thing. She'd kept it all a huge secret.

"What's this, a WI meeting?" Jack gave me a filthy look, shrugged his massive shoulders and then sauntered off back to the dressage arenas.

Sasha tore after him, sobs choking her voice, her hand reaching out, clutching at the back of his white shirt.

Zoe coughed nervously and started edging away towards the car park.

"How could you?" I spun round in shock and

disbelief. "Zoe Jackson, I don't believe what I've just seen."

"Oh well, that's you all over, isn't it?" she suddenly blasted out. "Too wrapped up in your own relationship to notice anybody else's. You're not my jailor, Alex, and maybe I don't want to go out with a geek. Maybe I want to go out with a real man, someone who's going places."

"The only place he's going is down the plug-hole. You've got no idea what he's like Zoe – he's a pig."

"You're just jealous."

"I am not." I was desperate now. I had half a mind to show her Dolly.

"Why can't you just be happy for me?" Zoe suddenly burst into tears. "I knew you'd be like this. Can't you see what's happened?" She looked at me imploringly, her face pasted in heavy make-up and a shine breaking out on her cheeks. "I'm in love."

CHAPTER NINE

Eric had disappeared. It was cross-country day and everything was chaotic. I'd overslept until 6.15 and padded out in my nightie to give Donavon his first feed.

I was a nervous wreck. Spectators were pouring in by the coach load and Daisy had chewed up most of Judy's "help" lists. It was boiling hot and there were already warnings going out on the loudspeaker about leaving dogs in cars.

It was 10.30 and Ash was due at phase A for roads and tracks in precisely twenty minutes. I stifled a panic attack and carried on trying to clean out Donavon's stud holes and plug them up with cotton wool. Someone had rock music blaring out on a radio and someone else was haring around asking for spare rubber reins. There was a great sense of camaraderie among the grooms and if it hadn't been for a girl called Sheila helping me with Donavon's weight cloth I think I would have curled up and died.

We were on time and we were organized. I flung a sponge, studs, brush and leg grease into a bucket for the steeplechase. Sasha led The

Terminator past. He looked absolutely fantastic and was jogging sideways eager to get on with the job. She was wearing dark sunglasses after spending most of last night in tears in Dolly's stable. I'd told her that after the cross-country during the late-night disco I was going to go to Sir Charles and tell him everything; that was if I couldn't find Eric first. I'd been to the members' car park and his green Fiesta which had occupied the only disabled parking space had disappeared. Nobody had seen or knew anything.

I was just fastening up Donavon's throat lash when Ash pounded in looking as wound up as a spring and clutching his jockey skull silk in his new colours, green and black. Sheila wolf-whistled as she walked past with a chubby bay and asked if Ash knew green was unlucky. I said he always wore odd socks, which should compensate, and Ash looked as if he was about to strangle me.

"Where's my jockey skull?" he demanded. "I've looked everywhere and unless you've buried it or used it as a portable loo I'm done for."

A cold grey cloud of realization settled on my shoulders as I remembered the cardboard box, all taped up, with jockey skull and a rubber gag which was still on the common room table, at home.

"Well don't just stand there, think," he bellowed. "You're always telling me you're the brains and I'm the brawn. Do something."

With legs like a greyhound I sprinted over to one of the tradestands, picked up the first hat I saw that was seven and a quarter inches and sprinted back to the stables still clutching Ash's wallet. I plonked it on his head and straightened his stock pin. "Now, are you getting in the saddle or are you going to twiddle around all day?"

Nerves were at breaking point as Ash launched off at a brisk trot to complete five kilometres of roads and tracks. Two women devouring strawberry ice creams immediately got in his way and one was convinced he was Jason Donovan. "Don't be so silly." The other stared after Ash's departing back. "It's Darren Day."

I was at the steeplechase course in plenty of time but desperately wishing I had someone there for moral support. I felt completely out of my depth and didn't really know what I was supposed to do. The gossip flying around was that a young blonde had streaked in the members' enclosure and had been led away wrapped in a horse blanket. I immediately thought of Camilla and then decided she wouldn't be that stupid. I'd last seen her chatting up Blake Kildaire over by the horseboxes.

Donavon came storming in after roads and tracks, fighting fit and hardly sweating at all. It was blisteringly hot and some grooms had stripped down to bikini tops.

The steeplechase was over a distance of about

three kilometres and had to be ridden at slightly less than racing speed, which was still incredibly fast, over solid brush fences – anything could happen. It was a bit like a Formula One racing car coming into the pits. Ash pulled up his stirrups and checked the girth while I screwed in square studs behind and sponged down Donavon's chest area and wiped behind his ears.

Everything was in place. Ash circled round, focusing his concentration, pulling down a pair of goggles to keep out the dust. He checked his stopwatch. News was coming in that the Farmyard Complex was proving a real bogey fence out on the cross-country and a couple of riders had taken a ducking at the water. Ash went from grey to stone grey and irritably asked what the hell he was doing here anyway. I fiddled with his back protector which just made him more volatile.

The loudspeaker crackled. "Number 48!"

Donavon powered forward, snatching at the bit, his bright chestnut coat sparkling.

"Five, four, three . . ." Ash tightened his reins.

"Two . . ." Donavon's whole body was bunched up, ready to spring forward.

"Go!"

They were off. A cloud of dust rose as Donavon's hindshoes dug into the baked earth. Within seconds Ash was a green and black dot streaking along the edge of the woods, hurtling over jumps, crouched forward, his hands moving in rhythm.

"Come on, Ash!" I dropped the steeplechase bucket and screamed at the top of my voice. It was exhilarating. It was so exciting I thought I was going to pop. Everybody's eyes were trained on the powerful chestnut horse with the big kind face and bold jump. Donavon reminded me of Aldaniti as he pounded along, giving it his best, answering Ash's every command.

"Way to go, Ash!" Camilla suddenly appeared at my side, all her blonde hair piled up on top and wearing a T-shirt which clung in all the right places and read "I love Blake". She had an Australian groom with her called Wally whose horse wasn't running until the afternoon so he'd offered to give Cam a guided tour round the cross-country. As long as that's all she wanted, I giggled to myself feeling euphoric as Ash blasted across the finish line.

Five seconds within the optimum time!

"No penalties." Ash fought to catch his breath, taking a quick swig of mineral water. I quickly sponged Donavon down between his back legs and his flanks to cool him down. His sides were heaving.

"Go, go, go." The steward was pushing him off on phase C. More roads and tracks.

"I'll see you at the ten-minute halt box," I

91

yelled, but he'd disappeared down a cedar track, pounding along between the ropes.

There were people scurrying everywhere. Two horses were out on the cross-country course and William McNally-Smith sounded as if he was going to be the first to go clear and within the time. Wally was fiddling with a stopwatch and I was desperate to get to the start of the cross-country course without forgetting anything vitally important and looking reasonably professional. Despite Cam continually talking and looking completely out of place I appreciated her support.

"Where is Eric?" I shouted, feeling perspiration running down my back. Temperatures were hitting the mid-twenties and I thought I was going to frazzle. Wally rubbed some suntan lotion on Cam's bare shoulders and I started deep breathing. This was where my help was desperately needed: the ten-minute halt before the cross-country was essential for checking over the horse, making sure he was as fit as possible, for the hardest section of all, the cross-country. Adrenalin was really buzzing now.

"Where is he?" There was no sign of any competitor coming in from phase C. The vet was hovering ready to do the final check. The closed-circuit television was flashing up pictures of a horse who had fallen at the water and been completely submerged for what seemed like ages. Another rider was retiring at the farmyard.

"They're dropping like flies out there." Someone was really acting as a confidence booster. Oh Eric, where are you when I need you most? I would have given a winning lottery ticket to see Eric and Daisy bouncing towards me full of advice and reassurance.

"He's here!" Camilla started leaping around, sloshing water from a bucket and accidentally kicking over my box of studs. "It's him! He's coming in!"

Donavon suddenly emerged from the trees, crashing along in an extended trot, his head perfectly bent, his tail held high. He looked absolutely beautiful.

"He's lost a shoe!" Ash was anxious beyond words. The vet and a blacksmith ran forward as Ash vaulted out of the saddle. "The near hind. It's ripped clean off."

Within seconds an emergency blacksmith was banging on a new shoe cold, nipping off the clenches, rasping down the toe. We had nine minutes to get sorted. Ash quietly walked up and down, gathering his thoughts, mentally visualizing some of the worst fences, making last-minute decisions.

Donavon stood patiently, despite being revved up and instinctively knowing what was coming next. Camilla held on to his reins while I pulled

93

the lid off the leg grease and started smearing it frantically on the fronts of his forearms, knees and leg protectors. If he hit anything the grease would help him slide over it.

Then I suddenly remembered I should be sponging him down first and I was doing everything back to front. With glued-up hands I grabbed a sponge and started sloshing water down his neck and in between his back legs and flanks. Wally came to the rescue, undoing the noseband and whipping off the saddle, rubbing him hard to remove the sweat and restore the circulation.

Seven minutes, thirty-five seconds.

The vet moved in for the inspection. I tried to trot Donavon up in a straight line even though my knees were quaking. It seemed a lifetime before he finally gave the nod and Donavon was through to the cross-country.

The temperature was rising. I splashed more cold water on his chest and rubbed his ears with a cold cloth. Wally had already fixed in the studs. Five minutes. Ten seconds.

Ash checked his stopwatch and prepared to mount. Camilla came racing up from a closed-circuit television in a nearby bar to say that if Ash landed over the bullfinch in six minutes, he could take the slow route through the Farmyard Complex and still be within the optimum time. As Cam was an ace at maths we had to take notice.

I checked Donavon's noseband and throatlash and Ash squeezed him forward into the box, ready for the countdown.

I picked up all my belongings and felt as if I was going to keel over with nerves and exhaustion.

Donavon immediately perked up and started twirling round and round. Ash looked straight ahead pinning his eyes on the first fence called a Flight Butt.

The starter moved into place, talking into a walkie-talkie. Apparently a fallen rider had delayed the off by about two minutes. Donavon broke into a sweat and started pawing the ground.

Jack Landers burst in from Phase C on The Terminator dripping with sweat and momentarily broke Ash's concentration.

"Five . . . Four . . . Three . . ." Donavon half reared.

"Two . . . One . . . *Go! Good luck!*"

They were off. I had never felt more nervous. People always say that watching is a hundred times more tense than actually competing, and as Donavon disappeared over the Flight Butt I felt as if I had my heart in my mouth.

Cam and Wally dashed after me as I desperately tried to locate a monitor which wasn't surrounded by vast crowds.

Suddenly there was a huge gasp and I immediately imagined that Ash had fallen and an ambulance had been called in. I grabbed a man in Union Jack shorts and demanded what had happened.

"It's all right." Cam was right behind me. "He's just had a sticky moment at the fourth fence – he's still going strong."

Ash Burgess and Jack Landers were both out on the course at the same time. It was bizarre. Please, Donavon, please do your best.

Wally elbowed a sea of people away from a television so we at least got a glimpse. Donavon was galloping in perfect style, meeting his fences just right, Ash keeping him between hand and leg.

Everybody whooped as it flashed back to The Terminator and Jack going like the clappers, not checking for anything. They were on course for the fastest time of the day and that would put them in the lead, if they stayed clear.

Ash had to go clear, just to stay in the top five. The pressure was on.

Cam was gripping my arm. "Come on Donavon, you can do it."

He flew over the elephant trap as if he'd got wings. "Steady, boy, steady." I was clenching my hands as if I was holding the reins, as if I was there riding, pushing on at a fast gallop towards the bullfinch. Five minutes, forty seconds.

"He's on course." Cam was ecstatic. "He can

do the time." We saw Ash check his watch and then kick on.

"That's my boy!" Donavon pricked his ears and leapt into space, skimming through the bullfinch and straightening up for the Farmyard Complex. Six minutes, eight seconds. "Come on my boy!"

Everybody suddenly hushed. This was the bogey fence. The last rider to take the direct route had been carted off to hospital. But Ash didn't need to do that. He had time on his side; we'd both analysed the alternative. Drawn diagrams. Ash had sat at our little formica table talking into a tape recorder going through each fence, describing the approach, gradient, angle and the best line. He'd played it back all night long even letting it run while he was asleep so it filtered into his subconscious. Ash knew exactly what was required.

I tensed and held my breath. The screen blurred slightly and then came back into focus. The Farmyard Complex had cost a fortune to build and was a mixture of gates, walls, hay racks and feeders; all massive and at difficult distances. The direct route was a bounce over two four-foot upright gates, a long stretch to a stone wall and then three short strides to a hay rack with two model Friesian cows placed one at each side. It was daunting. It was possibly unjumpable.

97

Ash sat bolt upright and guided Donavon off the line we'd planned. He was heading straight for the first of the farm gates. The commentator was going wild. Everybody stood pressed like sardines groaning or gasping in disbelief. Why spoil a perfect safe round? What was he thinking of?

I saw Donavon hesitate. Ash clamped on his legs. They met the first gate just right, then the second. Donavon grunted with the effort. He landed short and his next stride wasn't long enough. The wall was solid, big and unforgiving. He was miles off the perfect take-off.

"Go on!"

Every hind muscle strained with the effort. His knees scraped over the top, then he skewered to one side. Ash held him together brilliantly and pulled him onto a straight line for the hay rack.

It was the best part of five foot and not very inviting. The model cows were there to distract the horse from concentrating, to test just how obedient he was to the rider's aids. Ash gave the performance of his life. I'd never seen such a brilliant display of riding. He put Donavon in exactly the right spot and levered him up and over. There was a great whoop from everybody watching and somebody who was obviously taking bets started yahooing and saying he'd won the lottery. Donavon was the first horse to tackle the Burnley Farmyard Complex and his name was on everybody's lips. A reporter from *In The Saddle* who'd been huddled at the front suddenly grasped her tape recorder and hurtled off to the finish. Nobody took any notice of Jack Landers completing the slow route for a solid reliable clear.

The finish. I had to be at the finish for Donavon coming in. Completely forgetting my bucket I dashed off, tripping over both feet and hearing the roar of the crowds as Donavon cleared the last fence. I could hear over the loudspeaker that they were coming up the hill.

And there he was. Ash crouched forward, easing Donavon over the finish line and then thumping the air with his fist, a huge boyish grin breaking out on his glorious features.

As he slid from the saddle, undoing the girth, a TV reporter thrust a mike under his nose. I dashed forward and gave Donavon a big hug, undoing his noseband and lifting the reins over his head. Ten minutes, thirty-nine seconds. Within the optimum time and clear. Ash was a serious contender for the trophy.

"But anything can happen in the showjumping," I heard Ash say, still puffing and panting. "And it's certainly not Donavon's strongest point."

I walked Donavon back to the stables and washed him off, offering him a few sips of water at a time. Then I allowed him a few mouthfuls of hay before tackling the job of removing the grease from his legs and generally tidying him up. I was poulticing his lower legs and knees when Ash finally turned up, but with a face clouded with sadness rather than euphoria.

"What is it? What's happened?"

He took the lead rope from me and leaned his forehead against Donavon's nose. "Beautiful, good, lovely Donavon, you were a star today."

"Ash, there's something wrong. Tell me – you're frightening me."

He looked up, exhausted and just an empty shell. "You might as well know from me rather than someone else." He prized out a folded-up piece of paper from his jodhpur pocket. "You'd better read it. On second thoughts, sit down on that bucket first."

I took the piece of paper with trembling hands. Something was terribly wrong. I read the first thing I saw. Twelve thousand pounds. It was a cheque made out to Ash Burgess. In the corner was the signature and printed name of Sir Charles.

"That's right." Ash opened a bottle of lager. "I've sold him."

CHAPTER TEN

I couldn't believe it. Not Ash, not Donavon. They were made for each other.

"Don't look at me like that." Ash ran a hand nervously through his hair, staring out over the stable door so he didn't have to meet my eyes.

"Twelve grand will pay off my debts. It'll put me back in business. I'll be able to buy more horses."

"Oh yeah, and what about this horse?" I grabbed hold of Ash's hand and pressed it to Donavon's neck so he couldn't turn away. "He put you where you are today. Without him you'd be nobody."

Ash gently took the cheque out of my hand, folded it over and squeezed it into his jodhpur pocket. "Don't, Alex. Don't start – you know nothing about it. Sir Charles has promised . . ."

"Oh poppycock." I wrapped my fingers in Donavon's mane feeling his warmth and strength, wondering how on earth I was going to cope with leaving him behind.

Ash stifled a sob and put a hand over his eyes,

his mouth crumpling with emotion. "You've got no idea what this is doing to me."

All I could see was that he'd sold Donavon. "I never took you for a quitter, Ash." There were genuine tears in his eyes now. I'd never seen Ash cry before.

I pulled off my groom's badge and handed it to him, trembling like a leaf, flinching when he grasped my hand.

"I hope you can live with yourself," I gulped, "because I certainly couldn't. I wouldn't sell Barney for a million pounds."

"I'm not you."

"No, obviously not."

"Alex, come back. You're being stupid." But I'd already banged open the door and was marching down the line of stables towards Barney, biting back a fountain of tears. It was all over. No sponsor, no winning trophy, no Donavon. Nothing. Just blackness. An ugly great chasm of nothingness.

The disco was due to start at 9 p.m. There was always some kind of party after cross-country day and this time Sir James had organized a medieval theme and fancy dress.

Grooms and riders were milling round, shrieking and howling, dressed as knights, maidens, Lady Guinevere, even lepers and barons.

The last thing I wanted to do was dress up and have fun.

The disco struck up and three grooms came out of a horsebox wearing voluminous gowns and silly headdresses. Camilla came down to the stables with Wally dressed up as a knight and her own dress plunging daringly low. Zoe was last seen hanging out with Jack Landers' crowd who, according to Cam, were already dancing on trestle tables. She'd avoided me like the plague since I'd caught her kissing Jack, and Sasha had clammed up, just going through the motions of looking after Dolly and The Terminator. There was still no sign of Eric.

Ash was supposed to be meeting me at the main marquee at nine thirty after I'd finished the horses. But I had ideas of my own. I'd taken Barney for a long hack and I'd devised a plan of action.

The house looked empty as I walked up the drive in the evening, feeling small, insignificant and a bundle of nerves. Two carriage lamps were lit at the front door and there was a huge brass knocker in the shape of a lion's head. A butler opened the door, taking my name and asking me to wait in the sitting room which was huge and full of antlers and paintings of horses hunting, racing and playing polo. I floated across a Persian carpet and twiddled with my hands, trying to wet my mouth and lips which were as dry as the Sahara.

"I'll just tell him you've arrived." The butler disappeared, leaving me to my own thoughts and the nerve-stirring silence.

I was examining a picture of a polo pony called Calypso when the solid oak door creaked open and the man I'd come to see marched across with a huge hand extended and eyes tinged with a warmth which immediately settled my churning stomach.

"You're the girl with the dun pony who knows Eric Burgess, am I correct?"

"Yes, sir," I gulped, "and there's something very important that I've got to tell you."

"Well fire away. You've got my full attention." He sat down on a leather sofa and signalled me to a chair opposite.

I swallowed hard and felt my palms begin to run with sweat. "Well, Sir Charles, it's like this. It's about Jack Landers . . ."

The disco floor was a mass of gyrating bodies and flashing lights. A girl dressed as a nun was attempting to shimmy up a pole to release a clutch of helium balloons, and, over by the food, some girls were balanced on men's shoulders bashing each other with long strips of sponge. It was chaotic. There was no sign of Ash. Neither was there any sign of Cam or Zoe.

I stepped back out into the night air and decided to make my way to the horsebox to see if Ash was there. It was time I told him what was going on. There were some lights on in the stables where grooms were applying last-minute cold compresses to swollen legs. I pushed through the security gates and suddenly realized I hadn't got my groom's pass. The nightwatchman was standing waiting for me to approach, keen to see identification.

Just as I was dithering, wondering what to do next, someone grasped my arm and wheeled me round. It was Sasha and she looked frantic. "Where have you been?" she screeched. "I need your help. Jack's gone off his head!"

She was dragging me along, back towards the marquee and then on to the collecting ring in the far right-hand corner.

She was gabbling away in disjointed sentences, panic sweeping her face. Jack and his rat pack were drunk over by the practice jumps and were having a bareback competition. Darkness was descending fast.

"He's got Dolly," Sasha shrieked. "He's trying to jump her!"

Everyone was still over in the marquee, the music even louder. Someone pushed past me and then disappeared in the darkness. We could hear shouts and shrieks from the collecting ring.

"Come on," I yelled, running forward, desperate to find Dolly.

There wasn't enough time to get help. We were two girls against half a dozen guys according to Sasha's reckoning.

"You go on." Sasha lagged behind, gripping her ribs, as white as a ghost. "Save Dolly."

They were in the darkest corner by some trees, a guy dressed as a monk riding a big black horse over a single pole about four foot high – without a saddle.

A ginger-haired lad in a dress was the first to spot me. He hitched up his dress and lurched forward, obviously drunk. "Eh, it's National Velvet," he giggled. "Look at this, lads. We've got company."

Somebody else rode up behind me whistling.

"Where's Jack?" I lashed out, anger building up like a pressure cooker. "I know he's here."

"Eh lads, little Velvet's got spirit. Give us a kiss, love. I'm far better looking than Jack."

"Oh get lost." I pushed him down hard into the sand so he sprawled out on his bottom. "Now where's Jack?"

Dolly came skittering out of the gloom, shaking and sweating, Jack grinding her mouth shut by boring down on the reins. He was trying

106

to vault onto her back but she kept twirling round and round.

"Give over, you stupid cow." He lurched forward and smacked her hard right across the nose.

"Stop it, stop it, you moron." I dashed forward, grabbing hold of his arm, trying to unleash the reins.

"Jack, you're going too far." Zoe suddenly appeared, her hair stuck up like a hedgehog and wearing two tonnes of make-up. "I can't believe you're doing this."

Dolly backed up, clattered into a jump and then dived forward, petrified. Jack roared with murderous anger as she trampled over his feet and jabbed her so hard in the mouth that blood sprang to the surface.

"You ape," I screeched, leaping onto his back and tearing at his hair. He grabbed hold of my leg and squeezed it so hard I yelped. I bashed his head with my free arm and then he levered round and managed to get his hand round my neck.

"Alex!" Zoe was horror-struck.

I saw Sasha vaguely but Jack was spinning me round and digging his stubby nails into the soft flesh on each side of my throat.

I was choking.

Dolly broke loose, ran into the fence in blind terror and fell heavily on her side, heaving for breath. Sasha ran after her. Zoe came across to me and tried to prize off Jack's hands. He dumped me in the sand, flat on my back.

"You bitch," he spat in my face. "You interfering cow." He picked up a whip which had fallen in the struggle and held it above his head.

"Go on." I found my voice – I was fearless.

He was insane with rage, his mouth was flecked with saliva and his eyes were rolling like black marbles.

"Jack Landers, if you don't leave her alone I'll tear you apart limb from limb."

Ash bounded across the arena like a young Palomino stallion ready to fight to the death. I'd never felt more relieved in my whole life. Ash grabbed Jack by the shoulders and punched him square on the jaw and then in the stomach. The other riders seemed to have faded away into the darkness, smelling trouble. Zoe screeched at the top of her voice for them to stop but Jack had tripped Ash up and they were rolling around in the sand.

I scrambled backwards, my breath rasping. Sasha was desperately trying to calm Dolly who was rearing and plunging in manic fear.

"Stop it!" Zoe ran forward but got thrown off balance as Jack managed to get to his feet. This was the fight Jack had wanted for years.

"Ash!" Jack lifted up his knee ready to smash it under Ash's jaw.

"No!" Sasha let go of Dolly and pushed her way in front of Jack. "It's me, I'm the one to blame. Ash, I'm the girl on the moor." She pushed up her shirt sleeve to show an array of needle marks and turned back to Jack. "It wasn't Ash's fault. I saw. It was an accident. I've lied to you all these years. It was an accident."

She burst into tears, bowing her head and heaving with sobs. Ash stared at her in shock, hardly able to take in this new piece of information.

Jack's face was contorting. "He killed Cassie." He lobbed up some sand into Ash's face with his foot. Then he turned round and stared into the night sky, his shoulders shaking.

Suddenly a gravelly voice came from near the main gate. "He didn't kill anything." I could hardly believe it. It was Eric. He was back! He was trying to catch hold of Dolly's reins as she lurched towards him, dripping in sweat, almost threatening to jump over his wheelchair.

"Steady, girl, steady. There's my little beauty. Now now, come here." He made loads of soothing noises and instantly she calmed down, stood with her legs splayed, exhausted from fear.

"I saw the post mortem, Jack. It was heart

failure, there was an irregularity." Eric stroked Dolly's face, feeding her something from his hand.

"Liar." Jack backed up a couple of steps as if someone had slapped him across the face.

"Here, read this if you don't believe me. You wouldn't look at it at the time." Eric lowered some papers onto the sand. "Alex, come and help me with this horse. You need help, Jack, counselling. You can't carry on hurting other people. You need to get sorted out."

I moved forward mechanically and Ash followed. We trudged out of the gate and back to the stables, me leading Dolly and pulling my T-shirt up so Eric wouldn't notice the red marks on my neck. We left Jack, Zoe and Sasha staring at each other trying to sort out their feelings. I just prayed Zoe would now see Jack for what he really was and drop him.

Eric set to work on Dolly's injuries, getting Ash to fetch some cream from his car, all the while cursing Jack and running his hands over Dolly's legs, admiring her perfect conformation.

"She's a champion, isn't she?" I rubbed her gently behind the ears and patted her gorgeous neck.

"She'll do for me." Eric was besotted, it stood out a mile.

"I've sold Donavon." Ash blurted out the news. "To Sir Charles. I've got the cheque."

For a long time Eric didn't say a word. He just tensed around the shoulders and a muscle ticked erratically in his neck.

"Did you get a good price?"

"Oh for heaven's sake." I couldn't control myself any longer. "It's not about money, he should never have sold Donavon. You don't sell the things you love."

Ash whipped round glaring at me with red-rimmed eyes. "I can't live on fresh air, Alex. You're too romantic for your own good. You're not being fair."

"Stop it. This is ridiculous." Eric banged his arm on the wheelchair making Dolly jump out of her skin. "It's not over until the fat lady sings. Nobody knows what's going to happen."

"Eric, I've seen the cheque!"

"She's right." Ash moved towards the door looking desolate. "It's all over, Eric. If I won the lottery tonight, I wouldn't be able to get Donavon back. And without him there's no point. I haven't got the strength to go out looking for another horse."

"You don't have to," Eric answered. "This grey mare could take gold at the Olympics. She's got amazing potential."

"It's too late. Tomorrow will be my last competition. I'm hanging up my spurs."

"Leave him." Eric put a hand on my arm

111

as Ash stumbled out into the night, choked with emotion. "He needs to sort himself out. He needs time by himself."

Neither of us anticipated what was about to happen. We had no idea of the danger. We had no idea that Jack Landers still had unfinished business. And Ash was walking right into his trap.

CHAPTER ELEVEN

"He's gone!" I went back to the arranged meeting place, which was Barney's stable, in floods of tears.

Zoe, Cam, Wally and Eric were already there.

"Nothing, not a dicky bird."

Ash had disappeared. We'd scoured the whole showground and not found a trace. Neither was there any sign of Sasha or Jack. The showjumping was already under way and I'd had to take Donavon to the vet's inspection myself.

"Something's happened. Ash would never be this unreliable." I leaned back on Barney's door, trying to shut out the panic and failing. Something was terribly wrong, I just knew it.

2.30 p.m. We only had an hour.

"Unless he's done a bunk?" Zoe looked exhausted but insisted on helping with the search. She'd finished with Jack last night and had come running over to Dolly's stable in floods of tears. I'd won back a best friend and lost a boyfriend.

Barney butted me in the back and neighed wildly storming round his stable.

"That's it!" Wally, who up to now had been

really easygoing, suddenly became animated. "That little horse knows where he is!"

"What?"

"Honest. I've seen it before. I've got a brumby back home who's got a nose like a bloodhound."

"Wally, this is England." Cam looked exasperated. "Not the Aussie outback."

"I don't care, that horse knows something."

"Alex, get the saddle and bridle. It's worth a try." Eric was deadly serious. "Zoe, you get Donavon ready just in case he comes back."

Barney shot out of his stable on turbo power and immediately put in a volley of bucks.

"Let him have his head," Wally yelled. I pushed down my heels and we set off towards the car park.

Christy Mitchell had just gone clear in the showjumping with a young horse. There were ten riders left. "Come on, Barney, where is he? Where's Ash?"

The cross-country course was totally deserted; everybody was up by the showjumping. Barney burst into a gallop cutting across the steeplechase and heading for the woods. I could feel the excitement tingling through him. He belted on, then reached the edge of the woods and hesitated, stalking back and forth. "Where is he, Barney?" I gave him his head and wrapped my fingers in his thick mane. "Ash!" I started shouting.

Barney thundered off down a sand track. We were heading straight for the Farmyard Complex.

Then I heard a voice. It was Ash. He was yelling for help. We shot out through some pine trees and there he was. Tied up to the hay rack, trussed up like a turkey.

"Where have you been?" he grinned, looking terrible. "I thought you'd gone off with another man."

"Ash Burgess, you'll be the death of me," I grinned back, relief making my knees shake. "How on earth did you get tied up there?"

I jumped off Barney and ran across frantically pulling at the ropes and kissing him at the same time. "It's no good, Alex. I've sprained my ankle – you'll have to fetch help. I can't climb out of here. I can't even stand up."

"There's no time." The ropes came loose. "Barney will have to carry you out."

"Are you off your head? He's only 14.2. This hay rack's a good five foot."

"Ssssh." I kissed his dry but gorgeous lips and climbed back out.

"Alex Johnson, I forbid you to jump this fence."

Barney knew just what was required. I gave him a good straight approach, didn't even try to find a stride, just shut my eyes and kicked.

He took off. He landed way out the other

side and I had to yank on the reins to stop him flying over the stone wall.

"Right, Mr Burgess, let's give you a leg-up."

The pain must have been terrible. He looked as white as a sheet. I climbed back out shouting instructions to Ash. "Circle him and then give him his head. Don't lean too far back. Come on, Barney, you can do it!"

I backed up a few paces crossing my fingers. Ash looked enormous on Barney. His legs were dangling down past his stomach. "Think of Jack," I shouted. "Think of the Burnley Trophy."

Barney steeled himself for the task ahead. I was a wreck. From the ground the hay rack looked enormous. It was such a risk. If Barney fell . . . But Ash was a brilliant rider and he put him on a perfect stride. They were over.

I sprung up behind the saddle after giving Barney a mega kiss, grasped Ash's waist and clung on as we galloped back to the stables. It should have been romantic but all I could think of was Jack and how low he could stoop. Ash had to beat him. He had to climb on Donavon and jump a clear round.

Zoe was nervously leading Donavon around the collecting ring, tightening the girth. Eric was looking at his watch and pursing his lips. Suddenly Barney burst through the crowds, a yellow whirlwind, and I slithered off nearly landing in Eric's lap.

"Wally was right," I gasped. "Barney knew all the time."

Ash was in a worse state than we thought. He'd been left tied up all night by Jack and his sidekicks and his right ankle was blown up like a balloon.

"I don't care," he grunted. "I'm going into that ring."

"Over the brush fence first." Eric pointed to the course. "Then the planks, the wall, the spread, the open ditch – take care here, the ground's slippy. Push on after the double and make up time. Whatever you do, don't switch off for the last – it's big and it's running downhill."

Ash listened to every word. It was the first time I'd ever seen them so close. Zoe brought over Donavon. Cam was holding his black jacket and riding hat. I found some paracetamol in Eric's pocket but they most likely wouldn't work in time.

Ash looked on the verge of passing out.

Wally came back from the horsebox leading Daisy who was snuffling along the ground in her own little world until she spotted Barney and then went silly. We ended up with Barney and Donavon tangled up and Daisy wrapping her extendable lead round Eric's chair.

Then I spotted The Terminator walking round

the collecting ring, being led by the girl with white streaks. There was no sign of Jack, or Sasha.

"He'll never ride again after this." Eric was furious. "He'll be banned for life."

There was no time to think. Ash was due in next. He hadn't even warmed up.

"Good luck." Cam thoughtlessly squeezed his leg and Ash winced in pain.

"We're rooting for you." I blew him a kiss and held on to Barney who wanted to follow. Every time the audience clapped he thought it was for him.

"Set him up for the planks," Eric shouted.

The bell went and everybody fell quiet. Ash circled and approached the first at a steady canter. Donavon's great wafty ears were pricked forward in concentration. They always say big ears are a sign of honesty. Donavon could have been crossed with a donkey.

"Hold him." Eric was chattering away, but it was too late now. Ash was by himself.

The planks, the wall, the spread. A back pole rolled dangerously but stayed. Donavon started fighting for his head but Ash held him together. The pain must have been agony.

They steadied, turned, headed up the long side of the arena. I could barely watch. Ash looked as if he'd lost his way. All of a sudden he stopped dead in his tracks, got his bearings and then rode on. If he'd circled it would have been instant penalties. I stopped holding my breath and felt as if I couldn't take much more.

Now the treble. Another pole rolled. Still clear. Barney rested his head on my shoulder. Just the last. Donavon bowled along too fast, losing his rhythm. Ash fought to get him back. They were on the wrong stride. The front rail tipped out of the cup and it was all over. Five faults.

Ash rode out of the arena unable to talk for pain. Daisy had to be told off for getting under everybody's feet and Barney tried to chase after the next horse going in.

"It's not over yet," Cam was doing her mathematics. The commentator said the next horse had two fences in hand. I didn't see the round because I was too busy prising off Ash's boot. I think it was more than a sprain. It looked like a fracture.

"It's a cricket score." Eric was going wild. All three parts of the treble had come down, and the open ditch. "Ash, my boy, you're still in with a chance!"

Jack suddenly bounded across the collecting ring and vaulted onto The Terminator without warming up. He was the overnight leader.

"He'll be eliminated when I tell the authorities." Eric was adamant.

"We've still got to prove it," Ash winced.

"Nobody saw him tie me up. Nobody saw him beat up Dolly. Sasha's disappeared."

I realized he had a point.

The Terminator circled in front of the first fence, waiting for the bell. Jack was examining the course.

"He could eat up those fences. He could jump clear standing on his head."

"Ash, will you stop being so negative?"

I leaned against the ropes, trying to hide my anxiety. Jack looked hung-over and The Terminator seemed a little jaded. There was still hope.

"He's running on the forehand." Eric shuffled, on edge. "I can't see a thing – the sun's in my eyes." Cam passed him her flashy designer sunglasses.

The Terminator powered on to the planks. He wasn't getting the height. He was swishing his tail and shaking his head which was throwing Jack off a good stride.

Barney grunted behind me as if he could barely take the tension.

The spread, the open ditch. He was clearing them all. Then he turned downhill for the treble. Jack's hands were as stiff as concrete and I could tell The Terminator was getting more and more revved up. The crowd was clapping after every jump. It was becoming unbearable.

Jack set him up on a perfect stride, showing his technical skill as a rider. But suddenly on the last stride, The Terminator seemed to have had enough. He dropped his shoulder and veered out to one side, nearly unseating Jack and grazing the yellow wing.

"Yes, yes, yes!" Cam went berserk and threw off Wally's hat and then Eric hissed that Jack had three fences in hand. He could afford fifteen faults. We all fell silent.

Jack circled in a glacial temper and coldly put The Terminator at the fence again. Nothing. He dug in his heels and flatly refused to jump.

I drew in my breath and wanted to cross my toes. We were in with a real chance. Jack must have realized it as well. To the horror of the crowds he picked up his whip and started thrashing The Terminator round his head and ears and then sliced the whip back on his flanks so hard it must have cut through flesh. The Terminator spun round and round in growing terror trying to buck Jack off.

After a deathly quiet the crowd started booing. The noise rose to a crescendo and then the commentator announced over the speaker – elimination. Jack was asked to go straight to the steward's caravan for an official enquiry. Ash had won! Jack had shown his true colours in front of all the television cameras. Ash was the new champion. Ash?

He was leaning against Donavon's shoulder, choked up with emotion. Somebody led out The

Terminator, who was quivering with nerves and trying to bite anyone who came near him. I wondered how many other times Jack had hit him, how many beatings it had taken to ruin a good horse. Jack grappled through some ropes and stormed off towards the caravan.

Ash Burgess and Donavon were the new champions. It hadn't even begun to sink in. Other riders were coming up in hordes to shake his hand or pat him on the back.

Eric was fussing around getting Donavon ship-shape but grinning all over his face and still wearing the daft sunglasses. A newspaper photographer took a photo and Barney managed to push in his head at the last minute knocking over a pile of equipment.

"We've won!" Cam took the opportunity to give Wally a snog. Zoe gazed sadly at Jack's disappearing back and then snapped out of it when she caught me watching. "Plenty more fish in the sea," she shrugged. "Next time I'll try to be more discerning. Anybody got any food round here? I'm starving!"

Zoe Jackson was back on form.

"It's the prizegiving!" Ash groaned in colossal pain as we all heaved him back in the saddle and his ankle clanked heavily against the stirrup iron.

A nurse appeared with a medical bag asking

who was hurt but we said it would have to wait –
Ash had to do a lap of honour.

Barney was heartbroken that he couldn't go
in the ring, but momentarily stopped sulking when
he discovered a nice plant to eat.

Donavon looked wonderful in the ring. He
moved forward to accept the trophy, his bright
coat glistening in the sun. I was so proud I could
have exploded.

"Shoulders back, chest out," Eric told us, sal-
uting Donavon as he set off round the edge of the
ring.

We clapped as hard as we could and then had
to wait for ages while the photographers from
horsey mags took loads of pictures. Ash was going
to be famous. He was a rising star. Surely now he
couldn't give up eventing?

As soon as he came out of the ring Wally
helped him off to First Aid while I took Donavon
and Barney, one in each hand and headed off to
the stables. I still had my job to do as a groom
and I wanted to do it properly. Horseboxes were
pulling out from the main parking area, grinding
gears, heading home, riders in the cabs looking
enviously at Donavon's trail of rosettes. That's
when my happiness burst like a pricked balloon:
Donavon wouldn't be coming home with us, he'd
be staying here with Sir Charles. Ash had sold him;
he didn't belong to us any more.

123

I put Barney in Donavon's stable and tied Donavon up outside. A letter from Sasha was taped to the window.

Dear Alex,
Just to say thank you for your help with Dolly. I realize now that I don't have to stay with Jack. That he'll only sort himself out when he realizes he's got a problem. Eric has organized a job for me in a racing yard in Lambourn and I'm thrilled to bits. Hope all goes well in the showjumping.
Sasha

I was amazed. How did Eric know about Sasha's problems? What was he up to?

I untacked Donavon and washed him down with lukewarm water. Then I picked out his feet and applied a cool gel to his legs to take away any aches and pains. Then I washed his face and put on his travelling rug. All we could do now was wait.

"He looks beautiful." Ash was behind me, leaning on a pair of crutches, his face agonized as he gazed at the horse he'd owned since a foal.

"It's a chipped bone," he smiled as I looked down at his ankle. "Here, this is for you, for putting up with me, for working your guts out. You deserve it."

He handed me a box and inside was a gold pendant. It was inscribed *To my Alex, from Ash. With love*. It was gorgeous.

"Oh, I love you too." I threw my arms round his neck and kissed him passionately on the lips. "I hate it when we fight – I just can't bear losing Donavon."

"Alex."

"Yes, darling?"

"You're leaning on my foot."

I clung to him like a strand of ivy. "Isn't there any way we can get him back?" I whispered, starting to tremble as the sun disappeared behind some clouds. "If you don't mind I think I'm going to have to go and sit in the horsebox. I just can't bear it." I pulled away from him, looking back at Donavon one last time.

"Where do you think you're going?" It was Eric and he was pushing his chair straight towards us. Sir Charles was right by his side.

"What's going on here?" Ash stared at the two of them.

"Now then, old boy." Eric manoeuvred right up to Donovan and patted his neck. "Ready to go home?"

"W-what?"

Sir Charles burst into peals of laughter and thumped a great shovel-like hand on my shoulder.

"For a young slip of a girl you've certainly got some spirit."

"You've bought him." Ash worked out the secret before me. "What with? You've got no money."

"I beg your pardon?" Sir Charles rocked on his heels raising an eyebrow. "Is that any way to speak to your uncle?"

"Eric." I glared at him with mock-serious eyes. "What have you been up to?"

"Well, you know that old hunting painting above my fireplace?"

"Yes."

"It wasn't just any old painting. Old Charlie boy's been after it for years."

"We've done a deal. I've sold Eric this fine specimen of a horse and I've thrown in a little polo pony which I believe you're acquainted with."

"Dolly!" I jumped for joy.

"When you arranged for our private meeting, Alex," Sir Charles twinkled with mischief, "Eric here was in the next room and we were just finalizing the deal."

"So did you take any notice of me – about Jack?"

"I did my own bit of investigating and it seems Jack Landers is not all he seems. He's been prosecuted for cruelty in America. I doubt he'll

126

ever compete professionally again. So there's just the matter of who do I get to replace him?"

"Oh – Ash!" I screeched, unable to control myself. "He desperately needs a sponsor – he wouldn't let you down."

Ash promptly kicked me on the ankle and winced when it put a strain on his own.

"I think we'll be able to come to some arrangement." Sir Charles winked at Eric and then glanced down the walkway where Sasha was leading Dolly towards us.

"But I thought . . ."

"I haven't left yet," she grinned as she thrust Dolly's lead rope into my hand. "I wanted to see her with her new owners." Dolly gently put her nose in my pocket and rummaged for horse nuts. Barney stared over his stable door with adoration and infatuation. He was in love.

"This is unreal." I gulped back emotion.

Three days ago Ash had set out with one horse up for sale and no hope for the future. Now he had two champions and a sponsor – it was beyond belief.

Ash gave me a big hug and then saved one for Barney. Without him Ash would never have got back for the showjumping. Everybody was saying what I always knew – Ash was a rising star. And in eventing, with the right horse, anything was possible!

GLOSSARY

anti-cast roller   A stable **roller** which prevents the horse from becoming **cast** in the stable or box.

Badminton   One of the world's greatest three-day events, staged each year at Badminton House, Gloucestershire.

to bank   When a horse lands on the middle part of an obstacle (e.g. a **table**), it is said to have banked it.

bit   The part of the bridle which fits in the mouth of the horse, and to which the reins are attached.

bounce   A type of jump consisting of two fences spaced so that as the horse lands from the first, it takes off for the next, with no strides in between.

bridle   The leather **tack** attached to the horse's head which helps the rider to control the horse.

cast   When a horse is lying down against a wall in a stable or box and is unable to get up, it is said to be cast.

cavesson   The most-used, standard noseband.

chef d'équipe   The person who manages and sometimes captains a team at events.

colic   A sickness of the digestive system. Very dangerous for horses because they cannot be sick.

collected canter   A slow pace with good energy.

crop   A whip.

cross-country   A gallop over rough ground, jumping solid natural fences. One of the three eventing disciplines. (The others are **dressage** and **showjumping**.)

dressage   A discipline in which rider and horse perform a series of movements to show how balanced, controlled, etc. they are.

dun   Horse colour, generally yellow dun. (Also blue dun.)

feed room   Store room for horse food.

forearm   The part of the foreleg between elbow and knee.

gamgee   Material used under bandages to give additional protection and warmth.

girth   The band which goes under the stomach of a horse to hold the **saddle** in place.

Grackle   A type of noseband which stops the horse opening its mouth wide or crossing its jaw. Barney is wearing one on the cover of *Will to Win*.

hand   A hand is 10 cm (4 in) – approximately the width of a man's hand. A horse's height is given in hands.

hard mouth   A horse is said to have a hard mouth if it does not respond to the rider's commands through the **reins** and **bit**. It is caused by over-use of the reins and bit: the horse has got used to the pressure and thus ignores it.

head collar   A headpiece without a **bit**, used for leading and tying-up.

horsebox A vehicle designed specifically for the transport of horses.

horse trailer A trailer holding one to three horses, designed to be towed by a separate vehicle.

jockey skull A type of riding hat, covered in brightly coloured silks or nylon.

jodhpurs Type of trousers/leggings worn when riding.

lead rope Used for leading a horse. (Also known as a "shank".)

livery Stables where horses are kept at the owners' expense.

loose box A stable or area, where horses can be kept.

manege Enclosure for schooling a horse.

manger Container holding food, often fixed to a stable wall.

martingale Used to regulate a horse's head carriage.

numnah   Fabric pad shaped like a saddle and worn underneath one.

one-day event   Equestrian competition completed over one day, featuring **dressage, showjumping** and **cross-country**.

one-paced   Describes a horse which prefers to move at a certain pace, and is unwilling to speed up or increase its stride.

Palomino   A horse with a gold-coloured body and white mane or tail.

Pelham bit   A bit with a curb chain and two **reins,** for use on horses that are hard to stop.

Pony Club   International youth organization, founded to encourage young people to ride.

reins   Straps used by the rider to make contact with a horse's mouth and control it.

roller   Leather or webbing used to keep a rug or blanket in place. Like a belt or girth which goes over the withers and under the stomach.

saddle   Item of tack which the rider sits on. Gives

security and comfort and assists in controlling the horse.

showjumping   A course of coloured jumps that can be knocked down. Shows how careful and controlled horse and rider are.

snaffle bit   The simplest type of **bit**.

spread   Type of jump involving two uprights at increasing heights.

square halt   Position where the horse stands still with each leg level, forming a rectangle.

steeplechasing   A horse race with a set number of obstacles including a water jump. Originally a cross-country race from steeple to steeple.

stirrups   Shaped metal pieces which hang from the saddle by leather straps and into which riders place their feet.

surcingle   A belt or strap used to keep a day or night rug in position. Similar to a **roller,** but without padding.

table   A type of jump built literally like a table, with a flat top surface.

tack   Horse-related items.

tack room   Where **tack** is stored.

take-off   The point when a horse lifts its forelegs and springs up to jump.

ten-minute halt box   Area for enforced rest period between roads and tracks and cross-country.

three-day event   A combined training competition, held over three consecutive days. Includes **dressage, cross-country** and **showjumping**. Sometimes includes roads and tracks.

tiger trap   A solid fence meeting in a point with a large ditch underneath. Large ones are called elephant traps.

upright   A normal single showjumping fence.

Weymouth bit   Like a **Pelham bit**, but more severe.

Samantha Alexander

RIDERS 5

In the Frame

"It's you, isn't it?" I stared at the new groom with dawning horror. "You're the supermodel who's gone missing. You're Jade Lamond."

She pulled off her baseball cap letting ice-blond hair spill out to her waist. "If you tell anyone, you'll put Beachball's life in danger. Swear to me, Alex, swear you'll keep quiet."

But it's too late. Somebody has already rung the papers . . .